THE CONSEQUENCE OF LOVING ME

AFTERSHOCK SERIES: VOL. 1

KAT SINGLETON

This book is for every single person who cheered me on while writing this book.
I appreciate it more than I'll ever be able to put into words.
This debut is for you.

1

VERONICA

You don't drown by falling in the water; you drown by staying there.
– Edwin Louis Cole

UNLESS YOU ACTUALLY DROWN.

The college campus bustles around me as I stare at the quote in front of me. I have no idea who this Edwin guy is, but I decide in this moment that I hate him. He probably has no true experience with drowning. And using it as some sort of inspirational metaphor, when it *actually* takes lives, is just shitty.

No one *willingly* drowns. They aren't like, "Hey, I fell in this water. I think I'll just stay a moment." No. They get lost in the vicious movement. They get pulled under, sucked in, until they see nothing else—ever again.

I continue to glare at the sorry mistake of a self-help poster that's stapled smack dab in the middle of the bulletin board. My eyes narrow on it one last time before I notice someone standing next to me.

"You're looking at that bulletin board like it just told you Zac Efron is gay," he says.

I slowly pull my gaze from the offensive quote and instead focus it on the guy behind the voice. First, I glimpse at his shoes—a pair of white Adidas. One point for him; every other male on the campus wears boat shoes that their stay-at-home mother probably bought them last time she came to visit. I continue my trek up his body. Black joggers. White T-shirt. Chambray shirt casually strung over his shoulders, slightly wrinkled.

Finally, I make it to his face. He stares back at me, a lazy grin pulling at the corners of his mouth—a taunt.

He raises his eyebrows, nodding toward the paper. "It must say he's gay. Oh god, let me see." He steps closer to the board, consequently stepping closer to me, and reads the words in front of us.

I accuse him with my eyes as his sweep over the poster, patiently waiting for him to become uncomfortable, but it doesn't seem to faze him. "Every ex-Disney star or current Marvel heart-throb could come out as gay and I still wouldn't care. Hollywood is overrated."

He smiles as his hand runs over his mouth. "Said no girl ever."

My lips part in frustration. "Says this girl now," I counter.

He takes a small step out of my space. A disruption catches his attention across the quad, causing his gaze to flick in that direction for a small moment before he looks back at me. "So, since we came to the conclusion it actually wasn't because Zac Efron came out as gay, what did that poster ever do to you?"

Then, he reaches up and plucks the paper from the board. A small ripping sound mixes with the noise of a college campus at three p.m. on a Wednesday.

He reads the quote out loud, his thick eyebrows bunching together. "What's wrong with it? Cheesy, *maybe*, but inspiring."

I roll my eyes, letting out a sigh that's half-growl. "It's beyond cheesy. He's using something tragic like drowning to motivate college students. I don't know why he thought *anyone* would eat that shit up." The strap of my oversized purse starts to slide off my shoulder, so I shift my weight and pull it back into place.

He laughs, managing to annoy me more than he already has. "You are on a campus filled with a bunch of sappy young adults. *Everyone* eats this shit up. Everyone but you, apparently."

He neatly folds the piece of paper and tucks it into the back pocket of his joggers.

I glare at him before I turn back to the board, my lips pursing as I think about my plan of action. Finally, I swing my bag to the front of me and begin to rifle through it. My purse bumps against his arm, but to my dismay, he doesn't move. I finally find what I need—a flyer of my own, and the stapler I brought. I use one hand to hold the flyer up while my other staples it to the board.

Part of me was hoping Efron boy would have left me alone by now, but instead he uses this moment to step behind me and peer over my shoulder. My body tenses with his nearness.

"Looking for apartment or house available for rent. Not opposed to roommates. Call the number below if interested. Serious inquiries only. Veronica," he observes, his breath hitting my neck as he reads my words aloud.

He lingers on the last part—my name—dragging it out.

The heel of my combat boot makes a scratching noise against the floor as I hastily move back from the board and admire my handiwork. When I look down, I notice the paint splatters on my sleeve. If I cared what he thought of me, I'd be embarrassed.

He reaches in front of me and I watch in horror as he plucks the flyer from the board I *just* stapled it to. My mouth drops. "What the hell? I need that on there."

The guy chuckles, as he holds the flyer in his other hand. "Chill, *Veronica*," he says, dragging my name out again—and I hate it. "I'm just taking this off before a bunch of weirdos call you offering to be a bedmate, not a roommate."

I stifle the urge to hit him. There's just something about his smugness that infuriates me. And I consider if kicking his ass would be worth getting kicked out of school.

"Plus," he adds, "my roommates and I are looking for a new addition. It's your lucky day, Veronica! You can move in with us." His infuriatingly crystal blue eyes gaze at something behind my head before they once again focus on me.

"How do I know *you* aren't the weirdo trying to make me a bedmate and not a roommate?" I ask him. Disgust is clear in my tone and I don't try to hide it. My phone vibrates in the back pocket of my jeans, but instead of pulling it out to check it, I keep my stare aimed on him.

His eyes roam from the top of my head, down to my shoes, and back up again, unabashedly inspecting me. "Trust me, I don't want you in my bed. I do, however, want someone to help us cover the rent. Our last roommate fell in love with her professor and left without telling any of us."

To buy myself some time, I look around the quad, taking in the scene around me as I try to figure out the most polite way to tell him to fuck off. A tiny blonde cheerleader is thrown into the air by a man who looks like The Incredible Hulk from the corner of my eye. After watching her land safely in his hands, my eyes come back to the guy standing in front of me.

We both stare at each other, getting jostled by people passing by, until he moves. His fingers curl around my bicep. I have no choice but to move with him as he pulls me into the mass of people walking through our college quad.

His voice is way too close to my ear as he instructs, "Follow me. I need a coffee. But I want to figure out when you can move in."

"I never said I was interested in moving in with you." I yank my arm out of his grasp at the same time I plant my heels into the old concrete. People bump into me from all directions, but I stand my ground.

He turns around, raising his dark eyebrows at me. I wait for him to say something, but he doesn't. His shoulders rise and fall in a sigh as he also stops in the middle of the traveling bodies around us. We continue to stare at each other, and it's evident to me he has an iron will that rivals my own.

It's impressive, but not impressive enough to get me to move in with a complete stranger—an intolerable one at that.

I'm the first to break the silence. "I'm not following you. I don't even know your name. Plus, all you've managed to do in the few minutes I've known you is annoy me. We aren't off to the best start here." I scowl at another person who bumps into me while they rush down the sidewalk.

The stranger laughs at my reaction. It aggravates me. I let

out a sigh and turn around, walking back to the campus board. I try to think if I have anything in my bag that I can use to replace the flyer this guy decided to rip down. Just as I round one of the corners, I bump into a firm chest.

"Veronica?" a familiar voice says.

I look up to see the guy I hooked up with last weekend.

I think his name is Chad?

I can't remember, but I *do* remember that Texas accent that drawls out of his mouth. If the accent alone didn't speak of his hometown, the cowboy hat that sits on top of his head would give him away.

"Oh, hi," I respond, looking over my shoulder to find demanding roommate guy standing directly behind me.

Why won't he just take a hint already?

"I tried texting you a few times since we saw each other last," maybe-Chad says.

Or is it Brad?

It doesn't matter. I just really need to focus on not rolling my eyes.

Don't guys know it isn't cute when they're clingy?

And now, there are *two* clingers surrounding me—one I don't even know!

"Yeah, I got them," I answer Chad-or-Brad, lazily twirling a piece of my long blonde hair around my finger.

His eyes widen a bit. He obviously isn't used to being ignored.

Luckily, his phone rings from inside his pocket. He gives me one last inquisitive look before pulling his phone out of his pocket, then shakes his head and walks away.

I look back to clinger number two to find that taunt of a smirk still on his face.

"That happen a lot?" he asks, with humor in his voice.

I shrug. It does, but I'm not one to tell that to a *stranger*.

He holds out his hand while I stare at it questioningly.

His long, tan fingers wiggle in waiting. "My name is Maverick, by the way."

"Maverick," I repeat, not moving.

He takes a deep breath. "This is where you shake my hand and *not* make it weird."

For some odd reason—maybe manners, or the fact that he looks so desperate—I decide to take his hand. His large hand engulfs mine in a firm handshake, and I want to snatch mine back.

Instead, Maverick takes his back and proceeds to run it through the length of his dark brown hair. The items in his backpack move around as he shifts his weight. "So, back to our earlier conversation. Based on the awkward run-in you just had with our star pitcher Chad, and judging from almost every male's eyes in this quad, I see you *are* used to guys wanting to be your *bedmate*, but believe me when I say, I'm not one of them."

I finally roll my eyes, unable to hold it back any longer.

When I don't say anything, he adds, "Look, you seem cool—"

"You don't know me," I snap. At the same time, I feel my phone vibrate in my back pocket.

He's *still* annoying me, so I pull my phone out of my pocket to see who keeps calling me. My mother's name pops up on the touch screen. I swipe to ignore the call and toss my phone into my oversized bag.

He sighs as his fingers nervously tap against his thigh. The look on his face when his eyes rest back on me looks like *he's* the annoyed one now. "Look, I'm not going to battle a stranger to move in with us. We need a roommate to help take over rent, that's all. You're looking for a place. So, it seemed like a good fit. If you want to say no, that's fine. Or you can think on it. Maybe I'll see you around if you change your mind. In the meantime, I really need a coffee."

He begins to walk away, and just before he's engulfed into the crowd, I remind myself I *desperately* need a place to live, and then I yell his name.

He turns around, obviously waiting for me to make the next move.

"Oh hell," I mumble under my breath, just before I make my way to him. I wait to speak until I'm standing right in front of him. My head has to tilt up in order to look him directly in the eyes. "You have the time it takes me to drink *one* coffee to convince me that toying with the idea of moving in with you isn't a complete waste of my time."

His face is puzzled, like he isn't sure if I'm messing with him or not. A few beats go by where he doesn't say anything, but finally he gives one curt nod and politely says, "Follow me, Veronica."

This time, I don't have the same urge to strangle him when he says my name.

2

VERONICA

"SO, TELL ME ABOUT YOURSELF, VERONICA." Maverick rests his strong chin in the palm of his hand while his elbows rest on the old hardwood table.

I try not to roll my eyes again when he bats his long, dark eyelashes at me. He's obviously mocking this whole getting to know each other situation. And it's even more frustrating that he's undeniably attractive and seems like he knows it.

I take a long pull of my iced coffee, letting the bitter caffeine hit my bloodstream before dealing with him. "I'd rather not," I respond, the straw of my cup resting against my bottom lip as I look at him.

If my answer takes him by surprise, he doesn't show it. He looks around the small campus coffee shop. I analyze him as his eyes track around the busy building. I have been to The Roast at many hours of the day, and no matter if it's midnight or five in the morning, the place is always decently busy. It makes sense since it's the only non-chain coffee place within walking distance from campus.

Maverick's eyes narrow as he watches a guy put his arms around two girls. They giggle while the guy whispers something in both of their ears. Maverick is too busy staring down the guy trying to get laid to notice me. I fake a cough to bring his attention back to me.

His ocean-blue eyes land on me then, reminding me how much I hate the water. In fact, I loathe it. And I find it hard to look at him for that alone.

His narrow lips pucker together to blow on the coffee cup sitting in front of him. "I was waiting for you to tell me about yourself." His one eyebrow raises at me as he takes a sip.

Hating small talk, I sigh.

Does he need to know about the silver spoon I grew up with, permanently attached to my mouth? Or that I barely talk to my parents at this point? He definitely doesn't need to know that I can't even stand to look at myself in the mirror. Or that I push people away and pretend I don't care when I really do. Yeah, I'm not one for talking about myself.

I act like I'm thinking long and hard about my answer. Then, I make sure to look him in the eyes—the eyes that remind me of other things I don't want to talk about. My body shifts closer to the table, like I'm about to tell him a huge secret. My gaze quickly flicks to the womanizer across the coffee shop—who is now talking to two *new* girls—before it rests back on Maverick. I take the most dramatic deep breath and say, "My name is Veronica. And I need a place to live."

He laughs, but it isn't one of those laughs people let out because they feel uncomfortable or because they want to fill a silence. No—this laugh seems genuine. His skin wrinkles at the sides of his eyes as he smiles. The smile shows off perfectly straight teeth that no doubt cost his parents thousands of dollars.

What a shame.

I collect other people's imperfections. I cherish them when people have them.

I quickly try to find one of his, at least physically, but come up short.

He shakes his head while a lazy finger runs over the handle of his mug—not even gracing me with a verbal response.

A shrill laugh breaks my concentration on him. I glance over to where the guy from earlier pulls one of the girls onto his lap. It nearly causes her to spill some kind of ugly green drink all over both of them.

My eyes find Maverick once again. I wrap my hand around the cold cup of my drink. The condensation from it attaches itself to the skin of my palms.

He sighs. "I'll start then. My name is Maverick. I'm a senior here, majoring in poli-sci. Future lawyer."

Of course he is.

"I am originally from Kansas City," he continues, "which is only about forty-five minutes from here. My twin sister Lily goes here as well." He taps against the wood of the table, and I notice ink stains down the side of his left hand.

I briefly wonder if he's left handed as I take a long drink out of my straw. "Will she be one of my new roommates?"

His lips pull up in that taunt of a smile. "You say that like you're confident we'll take you in."

My nose scrunches. I shift in my chair, flipping my long, blonde hair over my shoulder as I say, "You say that like I'm a stray dog."

He lifts his shoulders in a shrug, a smirk forming on his lips. "Well if the shoe fits..."

I kick him under the table in the shin with the heel of my boot. He winces, immediately bending to rub where my heel just hit him. The sudden movement causes him to spill coffee all over his hand.

"Shit," he mutters, quickly dropping the coffee mug onto the table. It makes a loud *thump* in the process. He scowls at me while he licks the coffee off his fingers.

I give him an innocent smile. "I don't take well to being insulted."

He continues to clean himself up before he glances back at me, nodding. "Noted."

I sit back in my chair and hum, the smile on my face most likely making it blatantly obvious to him that I find joy in his displeasure. My fingers trace shapes on the condensation of my cup as I wait for him to clean up the mess he's made.

After he does so, the chair underneath him groans as he adjusts into a new position. "No, my sister is not one of our roommates." He takes a long sip from the mug then adds, "Lily and Aspen would literally kill each other if they shared the same roof over their heads."

"Aspen?" I ask.

"Veronica, meet Aspen." His long finger points to a different corner of the shop, and my eyes follow it.

I can't help but be a tiny bit surprised when I notice the guy from earlier. He still has the one girl from earlier placed in his lap as he laughs with one of his friends.

"That man-whore over there is my best friend, and unfortunately, my roommate," Maverick clarifies.

"You can't be serious." Color me actually shocked. Somehow it didn't even occur to me that Maverick would be friends with someone like this *Aspen* guy.

Then again, I hardly know Maverick. And I certainly don't know his obnoxious friend. But something tells me Aspen is more of an open book than my good friend Maverick here is.

Maverick chuckles as his hand runs through his hair again, simultaneously showcasing the lean muscles that wind up his arm while I fight another eye-roll at what seems like a display. "Unfortunately, I am dead serious," he says. His gaze travels to where Aspen finally takes notice of the two of us across the coffee shop.

I stare in disbelief—*or is it fascination?*—as Aspen deftly shoves the girl off his lap and crosses the space. "Maverick!" he calls.

Aspen's long legs take him quickly across the coffee shop. I'm not shocked to find a pristine pair of boat shoes attached to those legs. Maverick stands up to do that odd greeting guys do before Aspen plops down in a chair too close to mine.

"And who is this beautiful creature?" Aspen asks, his arm stretching out to rest on the back of my chair.

My chair makes a loud screeching noise as I push it farther away from him. "Uninterested," I state.

I stare him dead in the eyes before the biggest grin spreads over him. The smile takes up so much of his face. I wait to see what his reply will be, but he just shakes his head and whispers something to Maverick.

My eyes cautiously watch them exchange words. The two are different in many ways. Maverick has a calm, confident demeanor about him. From the ten minutes I've already observed Aspen, he has more of an in-your-face air of confidence. Maverick's dark hair is longer on the top, buzzed at the sides. Aspen's is blond and buzzed all the way around his head. As I stare at Aspen, I notice his face is made of soft edges, like his peaked nose. Maverick's face is completely made of straight lines and hard edges. I begin to compare their eyes when I realize Maverick is staring at me. The corner of his lip pulls up when Aspen says something else in his ear.

I huff in response. "Care to enlighten me on what you boys are talking about?" My coffee makes a slurping sound as I finish the rest of my iced latte. I shake the ice around to try to get one last sip of the caffeine before I plop the cup back on the table.

"I was asking my good friend Maverick about *his* new friend." Aspen waggles his eyebrows.

Maverick stays still.

Yup. Very different.

Deciding *what the hell*, I stretch my arm out in Aspen's direction. "Veronica Cunningham. Can't say it's too nice to meet you."

His eyes light up like those of a dog that's just had a bone placed in front of him. He takes my hand in his and shakes it. "Aspen Bellevue. And I *can* say it's nice to meet you."

His fingers latch around my hand. I decide I've been nice enough for one day and pull my hand back, setting it in my lap.

"Veronica here is going to be our new roommate," Maverick chimes in.

He's been so quiet during this encounter I almost forgot he was there.

Aspen's eyes shoot to me as he ponders over his friend's words. "I think my year was just made."

Maverick shakes his head as he takes a casual sip of his coffee. His phone vibrates on the table and he quickly reads over the words.

"This will be interesting," I exhale, not quite sure what I'm about to get myself into.

I expect Maverick to comment on the fact I had just *pretty much* agreed to move in with them, but he stays fixated on the iPhone he holds.

"Everything okay with Selm?" Aspen asks, a serious tone taking over his just-playful voice.

One of the girls who'd previously occupied his lap starts to walk our way across the shop, but after one serious look from Aspen, she turns around and sits back down with her group of friends.

Maverick's eyes catch mine for a brief second before he pushes his phone into the pocket of his joggers. "I gotta run. Aspen, will you get Veronica's number so we can set up a day for her to move in?"

Aspen nods, a concerned look written all over his face.

My jaw hangs open as I wonder what the hell is going on.

And who is Selm?

Maverick reaches across the table, laying his cold fingers across my hand that's sitting on the table. "It was nice to meet you, Veronica. Looking forward to having you in our place."

And with that, his tall body gets up from the small chair and walks out of the coffee shop, while I'm left staring at his retreating form. My thoughts are all over the place, and I'm unsure *which* exact part of the last hour to process first.

Why does Aspen look so concerned?

Am I really about to move in with complete strangers?

All these thoughts cross my mind as I type my number into Aspen's phone. He's saying words to me, but they aren't registering.

Finally, I catch a mumbled *goodbye* from Aspen before he gets up and heads in the direction Maverick just went.

Well, this just got even more interesting.

3

MAVERICK

"I'LL BE THERE in five minutes," I tell Selma, hanging up the phone and quickly dodging a person on a bike who almost just trampled me. My tennis shoes scratch against the pavement as I rush toward the fine arts building all the way across campus.

I pass by the message board where, just over an hour ago, I first met our new roommate—Veronica.

It's odd to think I was mere seconds away from missing her when I left my last class for the day. She was standing there, staring at the board, and for some reason, that—in combination with her pink floral combat boots—got my attention.

The slightly tense introduction led us to where we are now—me, possibly having a psychopath as a roommate. Judging by her long blonde hair, know-it-all attitude, and sarcastic quips, something tells me this may have been a mistake. But, we need a roommate.

At least she doesn't smell.

There is the small matter of Aspen already falling for her just by what she looks like. He'll learn as quickly as I did that there's something more behind her pretty face, and I'm not sure it's exactly pleasant. A small price to pay to have someone chip in on the rent.

I find Selma crying outside the brown brick fine arts building. She's huddled behind a bush that looks like it's only days away from completely dying. When I put my hand on the small of her back, she flinches under my touch, a breath of air flying from her lips in a gasp.

Her green eyes connect with mine, and my heart breaks inside me as tears fall down her pale cheeks.

"I didn't realize it was you," she says, sniffling. She uses her sweatshirt sleeve to wipe under her eyes, smudging mascara across her cheekbone in the process.

I reach up and gently use the pad of my thumb to wipe it off. When I take in the rest of her body, I notice her other hand is clutching her phone, her already pale fingers turning paler. I gently pry her fingers open and put her phone in my pocket.

"Come here," I say, pulling her into me as close as possible. I would swallow her whole if it meant I could protect her from the rest of the world.

Her small body molds around mine as she lets out a sob.

My hand gently strokes her short, auburn hair, my fingers tangling through her unruly curls. We've been in this same position many times before, and I know there's nothing I can do for her other than stand here and be her strength.

I've been Selma's rock since we were kids; since her family moved in next door and I witnessed her dad chastise a seven-year-old about the way she was carrying a box. It was a bright sunny Kansas day outside, but her face only reflected darkness —sadness. There aren't many memories I have of my childhood that don't include her. For as long as I've known Selm, I've been her safe place. Her home. Because the actual home she comes from is her own living hell.

"I hate him," she says against my abdomen. It comes out muffled, and her hot breath against my abs sends shivers down my spine.

"I know, Selm," I respond. "I do too."

She's talking about her sorry excuse of a father. It takes a lot for me to dislike somebody, and I rarely use the word *hate*, but I hate Tony Matthews with every fiber of my being.

He's the reason Selma constantly cries, even though I've done everything in my power to shift his fury away from her. Since I was a kid, I've made it my job to put myself between

Selma and her father; and every time I think I've succeeded, she somehow still ends up in tears. My armor has taken many blows from him. I was Selma's knight in shining armor before I even knew what that meant, and I won't stop being it now.

I continue to play with her hair, clutching her tiny body against mine. We fit together like an odd-shaped puzzle—her petite frame almost too small for my tall one—but somehow, we make it work. That's the story of *us*—making it work, despite every obvious thing insisting we shouldn't.

Finally, her crying subsides, and her heart-shaped face looks up at me. Her green eyes glisten as she whispers, "Take me home?"

"Always," I respond, bending down to kiss the top of her head. I stay there for a moment, lost in the comfort of her scent. The same scent she's had since I first kissed her in high school.

We walk in silence at first, both too wrapped up in our own thoughts to create conversation. I have to slow down my steps so her short legs can keep up. Once we're a few minutes away from our house, I finally get the balls to ask her what happened.

When she doesn't answer, I run my thumb over her small hand in mine. "Talk to me, Selm."

She doesn't respond at first, and I give her the time to work through her thoughts. Just when I think she might not tell me, her soft voice speaks. "He found out I got a B on my comp two paper. He's pissed."

I nod, running her words over in my head.

Selma is an only child to a father who runs one of the biggest law firms in the state. His dream was to have a boy who would one day run his company for him. I wouldn't have wanted to be in the hospital room when he found out the boy he'd been told they were having the whole pregnancy was actually a girl.

He's resented Selma her whole life. Since the moment she took her first breath, he hated everything about her. Starting with the fact she was a *her*.

In short, he's a dick.

Selma's mother, on the other hand, was the kindest human being I knew—until she changed. As we were growing up,

Selma's mom—Tiffany—radiated kindness. She was constantly in the kitchen, baking anything my five-year-old brain could conjure up and request. She was the icon for local philanthropists. She held charity functions all the time. Selma and I were constantly going through her toys to donate to children who weren't as fortunate as we were.

Tiffany Matthews had the kindest soul.

But Selma's dad—Tony—can tarnish anyone he meets.

Now, Tiffany is harsh. Cruel. She might even say worse things to Selma than Tony does, at this point.

I remember the moment I realized Tiffany's heart went from being soft to harsh. Selma and I were both fifteen, and it was just before our school homecoming dance. I had arrived early, and I sat in Tony's office for fifteen minutes as he dragged on about his firm. Part of me was interested—by then, my dream of becoming a lawyer had only just surfaced—but a bigger part of me was wondering when Selma would save me from her dad.

Finally, I heard voices in the kitchen. Tony and I both made our way in that direction. Selma and I were positioned in front of their spiraling staircase, my arm draped modestly around her waist. It was the closest she and I had ever been. I could feel her quick intakes of breath where my hand rested above her hip. I was lost in thought—realizing my palm had never rested on a girl like this, let alone my best friend—when Tiffany's words broke through my thoughts.

"Selma, dear?"

"Yes, Momma?"

"You need to suck in. I can see way too much of your fat in these photos," Tiffany said.

My hand felt the way Selma's stomach tensed. And worse, I felt her stomach pull in.

"Much better," her mother said.

Because of my hand placement, I knew Selma spent the next five minutes of our photo ops with her stomach clenched and pulled in. I spent those same five minutes with my blood boiling.

Her mother had gone cold, and I knew it had to be devastating for Selm.

It was a pivotal moment in my life. Before then, I had always protected Selma; it was in my blood to do so. An instinct. But on that day, I vowed to myself that I would *never* let Selma's kind soul turn to stone like her mother's had.

I wouldn't let her father *or* her mother be the reason the light left her eyes. Nothing else mattered to me in that moment other than sheer determination to wrap Selma in a tight cocoon and use myself as a shield to protect her from the harsh reality of her world.

That night was the first night I kissed her.

It was the night we went from being *best friends*, to being *more*.

Now, our *more* looks a lot like *best friends who share a bed and occasionally kiss every now and then*.

Selma's voice breaks me out of my memory. She's going on and on about how hard she studied for the test, which she did. Every spare second she found—outside of work and completing her assignments for her other classes—had been spent studying for that test.

But to her dad, it didn't matter.

"He has no right to be mad, Selm." I reach into my pocket and pull out the keys to our front door. They jingle before I twist them in the appropriate locks and pull them back out.

Selma barely looks at me as she breezes in, letting her backpack flop onto our couch when she reaches it. "But he does, Maverick. He's paying for me to go here. I don't want to disappoint him. I just need to work harder. Be better."

Her last words are said from the kitchen. I hear her open the refrigerator door and rifle through it until she finds whatever she's looking for. Probably string cheese. She's been obsessed with it since we were children.

I find my guess to be true. She's unwrapping a cheese stick when I walk into the kitchen.

I prop my hip against the granite counter and look at her. "Want me to talk to him?"

Her small fingers pull a long strip of cheese and then she places it into her mouth. Those green eyes find mine as she nods her head.

"I'll call him right now," I respond, pulling out my phone and retreating to our patio.

His name is in my recent call log, so I click it and wait for him to pick up.

We're a couple of minutes into a heated conversation when Aspen approaches our house. I can tell he knows exactly who I'm talking to by the look on his face. He gives me a sad nod before going through the front door. I know Selma's in good hands with Aspen, so I engage again with Tony.

"I won't accept an illiterate daughter," he says, causing blood to rush through my body in anger.

"It was a B, Tony. She worked her ass off and studied hard for that test. Give her a break," I tell him, trying to reason with the man.

"That doesn't help her case. If she worked as hard as she said she did, she wouldn't have gotten a B."

My eyes wander to my black joggers, where I find a long blonde piece of hair. It must be Veronica's. I hold it between my two fingers and let it fly away in the wind as Tony continues to drone on.

"How are your classes going for you, Maverick?" The tone of his voice changes when he asks this—because he respects me.

And it only disgusts me. Selma longs for the exact thing I receive from him so easily. But, that same respect is also an advantage for me. It helps me turn his anger away from her.

"Going well. I've been spending a lot of time in the library, but it's paying off." My eyes follow a group of students walking down the sidewalk in front of my house.

"I'm glad to hear that. Don't disappoint me, my boy," he says.

"I won't, sir. But I need you to give Selma a break. She's been working hard." Somebody's voice echoes on the other line, and I know that voice is his secretary—Amber. The same secretary that is way too young for him, but somehow, he's still having an affair with.

I've interned at his law firm the last two summers, and anybody with a pair of eyes can see they're hooking up.

"I gotta go, Maverick," he rushes out.

And just like that, the line goes dead. When Tony Matthews wants off a call, it's over. There's no exchange of pleasantries or long goodbyes.

I sit outside for a few minutes after we end the call, gathering my thoughts. My mind runs over how much of that conversation I want to tell Selma. He's said enough harsh things to her today, and I won't let her hear any other negative things tonight when it comes to her as the subject.

My body lets out a long sigh as I stretch in the chair before getting up. When I walk back into the house, Aspen is enthusiastically rattling on about something.

"She's the most badass chick I've ever come into contact with, Selm. I mean, my charm had *zero* effect on her. In fact, I think it pissed her off. I'm in love." His hands are flying all over the place as he talks.

Selma giggles from her same perch in the kitchen.

"I can't believe I'm going to be living in the same house as her," Aspen says. "This is my wildest fantasy. Oh my god, what if I see her in the shower?" His hand goes over his heart as he mimics a dreamy look on his face.

I throw the closest thing I can find—a dish rag—at him.

"Aspen here is telling me we have a new roommate. *Veronica*," Selma explains, pulling her hair up into a ponytail. She expertly winds a hair tie off her wrist and spins it around her hair.

"Where did you even find her, Maverick?" Aspen asks, his hand still resting on his chest.

Both Aspen's and Selma's eyes find me, each obviously waiting for an answer.

"It happened kind of randomly," I begin, letting my body fall onto our gray couch. I explain the chain of events, and how it seemed like it'd be a good fit.

"I hope I'm a good fit," Aspen retorts, grinding his hips.

"Gross," Selma's soft voice says, not hiding the laughter.

"I'm so happy you happened upon that beautiful creature, Maverick." Aspen looks at me like I just gave him front row seats to a Kid Motto concert.

I shake my head at him. Veronica and I only spent a short

time together, but somehow, I knew Aspen was going to be very let down by her. She has bars around her made out of Valyrian Steel, and I don't think anybody's going to easily penetrate those walls—let alone Aspen.

My mind replays the events of the day and how exactly I ended up with Veronica as a roommate despite her rubbing me the wrong way after knowing her for only an hour. I'm still unsure how things will unfold with her. She and I may end up at each other's throats, or it may be that way with her and Aspen —maybe both.

But I am sure of one thing. Our new roommate seems like there's a *lot* more to her than what meets the eye—and I want nothing do with it.

4

VERONICA

Two DAYS GO by before it's time to see Maverick and his obnoxious friend again. When we spoke last, we agreed I would bring some stuff over after my shift at the art gallery I work at. I currently have two hours left of my eight-hour shift, and my feet already hurt from the ridiculous pair of heels I decided to wear.

I welcome the pain of the shoes. It's a distraction from everything else going on in my head.

My boss—Clementine—yells at me from across the studio. "I have someone coming in twenty minutes to pick up a piece they bought. Will you make sure everything is handled accordingly with them? If all goes well, I'm hoping they buy more from us as they decorate their vacation home in the Hamptons."

My fingers type loudly across the keyboard as I construct the latest social media post for the gallery. I give her a quick response before going back to finishing the post.

In twenty minutes on the dot, a man in his late fifties walks in with a woman who looks to be only a few years older than me on his arm. Standing up and smoothing out my skirt, I walk across the marble floors to greet them. "Welcome to Clementine's Art Gallery. My name is Veronica. How can I help you today?"

I want to crawl out of my skin as the man's eyes roam over

my body for way longer than necessary. I look at the woman next to him, wondering if she realizes the man she's with is obviously a perv. She's too busy typing away on her phone to notice him. Every part of me wants to bite this man's head off for looking at me the way he is, but instead, I give him my sweetest smile as I wait for his eyes to meet mine once more.

"Hello, dear," he finally says.

Gross.

"I'm here to pick up a piece," he states. "Clementine said it would be ready for me."

"Yes, it is ready for you. Let me get the paperwork and it'll be all yours," I tell him. My shoes echo loudly off the floor as I return to the front desk. I already prepped his paperwork, so all I have to do is hand him the clipboard.

As he reads it over, I head to our back room and retrieve the piece he bought. I almost laugh out loud when I realize he purchased the piece Clementine bought from someone at a music festival when she was probably high as a kite. The whole time it's been on display at the gallery, I've thought it was hideous, but apparently it just needed someone a bit more pervy to appreciate it. The piece is made up of strategically placed blobs that very clearly make a shape that looks a lot like a woman's lady bits.

Art is my jam. I live and breathe it. I admire the piece as I wrap it up nicely before bringing it out to the creepy old man and his way-too-young girlfriend.

After they leave, the rest of my shift drags on. I feel the itch to be deep into my paint set with a canvas in front of me. However, I find myself robotically replying to potential customers on social media.

Finally, the clock reaches four and I give Clementine a brief goodbye before I shoulder my large purse and am out the door. My heels click against the cobblestone downtown sidewalk. When I reach my car, I throw my purse in the passenger seat and unhook my parking pass off the rearview mirror. I already know the location of the house I'll be living in, so I turn on my music and head that way, knowing I'm about to find out if saying yes to Maverick was a good decision on my part or not.

Between Maverick's cold, indifferent demeanor and Aspen's overeager personality—my bet is on the latter.

5

VERONICA

I PULL up to the house seven minutes later. It's a nice, short drive from the gallery, and walking distance from campus. Each are a plus. When I look up, Maverick is sitting on a balcony, staring down at me. We stare at each other for an awkward moment before he pulls himself out of a lawn chair and slides the patio door open. My eyes stay on the empty porch for a few moments longer before I return to reality. Footsteps sound on the stairs as I lift my purse from the passenger seat. When I open my car door, Maverick's heading in my direction.

His eyes fall to the five-inch heels I have on. He shakes his head. "I was gonna ask if you needed help carrying anything, but I'm almost tempted to let you do it alone just to see if you can manage it in those things."

My eyes narrow at him. I am fully equipped for this. My mother had me in heels before I even started high school. I could probably run a marathon in these things. No doubt my feet would be hurting, but I'd be damned if I couldn't do it. "You need to learn one thing right now, Maverick. I can do anything in heels. And I'll look damn good doing it."

My feet reach pavement and steadily find themselves on the cracked driveway. With heels on, I'm more eye level with all at least six feet of him than I was the other day. I give him a pointed stare before stepping past him and opening my trunk.

"I thought you said you were only bringing a few things," he states, his body now next to mine as his eyes roam over my filled-to-the-brim trunk.

My hand reaches in for a large duffle bag. "Oh, this is a few things."

Maverick shakes his head again, making the top of his hair fall over his eyes, when a voice comes from the house.

The look on his face makes me wonder if he regrets asking me to move in. I'm about to ask when I hear the voice again.

"Where's my future lover at?"

When my eyes follow the direction of the voice, I find Aspen standing on the porch with a tiny brunette next to him. I let out a sigh, wondering if I can live with this kind of man.

He's calling me his future lover with his current lover standing right next to him? Really?

"How about you stop drooling over our new roommate and come help me bring in her things? Apparently, *a few things* actually mean *a carload*," Maverick shouts from behind me, his statement carrying a disgruntled tone.

He sidesteps me and starts to climb the stairs to the front door, not giving me a second glance.

My feet steadily take the concrete stairs before I stand at the threshold of what is my new home. Assuming it's okay to walk right in, I do just that. I'm met with a nicely furnished house that definitely does not look like it belongs to two guys almost out of college.

It has a feminine touch to it.

And just when I'm wondering whose touch it belonged to, the brunette from earlier slides the patio door closed and walks toward me. She's beautiful. Every part of her screams kindness and even my cold, black heart smiles back at her as she crosses the room. She takes a moment to set her phone down on a gray ottoman before closing the distance between us.

Maverick comes out of a door that must lead to my room, considering his hands no longer hold the boxes from my trunk. He leans a shoulder against the door frame, his stare locked on the girl in front of me.

My focus returns to her just as she opens her mouth to speak.

"Hi!" Her voice is as sweet as sugar. It sounds like it belongs in a commercial selling something girly and nice. Her hand extends between us, and I don't hesitate to take it as I wonder who exactly she is.

"I'm Selma," she says. "Mav's girlfriend."

My gaze automatically locks on Maverick, who's standing behind her. But when I look at him, I don't see any emotion on his face. He just stares at the space between me and his girlfriend.

"It's nice to meet you, Selma. I'm Veronica." I give her a genuine smile, because she seems too nice to receive a fake one.

Aspen opens the patio door as he exchanges goodbyes with someone on the phone. He dodges a loveseat close to the patio door as he literally swaggers in our direction. "Welcome home, girl!" he exclaims.

Then, he wraps me up in a very unwanted hug that involves my feet leaving the floor. My duffle bag makes a loud *thud* on the hardwood floor as it falls from my grasp in the process.

"Let's not scare our new roommate, Aspen." Selma giggles as she smacks Aspen on the arm.

Her words influence him enough to put me safely back on the ground. His arm, however, stays around my shoulders as I listen to Selma tell me about the house.

As she explains the living area, I take the time to look around. After walking through the ugly green front door, I'm met with a decent sized living space. There's a large gray sectional pushed up against the wall, decorated with throw pillows. That was my first cue that a female lived in my new humble abode. It's apparent males live here, though, by the giant flat screen attached to the wall. An informercial about vacuums plays on the screen. Selma continues to ramble on—this time about groceries—as I scan the kitchen.

The kitchen is small, but it has updated appliances. In the corner sits a small white table with four teal chairs surrounding it. I make a mental note to find myself with other plans if they ever ask me to eat with them in the small space. There's also a bar separating the living room from the kitchen. Three perfectly aligned barstools sit in front of it.

"Veronica?"

Hearing my name snaps me out of my thoughts, and I search for the speaker.

"Want to see your room now?" Maverick repeats.

Selma's eyes ping pong between me and Maverick before she bends down and grabs my duffle bag from the ground.

I nod, muttering a quiet *thank you* to her as I pick up my purse.

Maverick's body retreats down a set of stairs that open up to a basement. Aspen stands a little too close to me as I make my way down and look around.

A pool table sits in the middle of the room. It looks well loved, and apparently a game was cut short, because balls are still scattered around the table. Two pool cues lean against the table, haphazardly propped up. As we walk through the basement, we also walk by an old card table that looks like it's seen better days.

Finally, we make it into what will now be my bedroom. I have to admit, it isn't so bad. I'm used to a king-size bed, but considering I'm trying to get *away* from my parents and their money, a queen will do.

It's pretty bare in the room. It seems that even though their last roommate ran away with her professor, she still took everything but the bed and a dresser. The dresser sits across from the bed and a full-length mirror is perched on a stool next to it.

Selma sets my duffle bag on the bed, saying there are extra sheets in the linen closet upstairs. The boxes Maverick brought in earlier sit next to what looks like the door to the closet.

"The bathroom is out there," Selma explains, pointing to the living area in the basement. "I will warn you, the boys come down here a lot. I try to force them to use their own bathrooms upstairs, but they don't listen." Her green eyes burn right into both Aspen and Maverick.

Maverick shakes his head, giving her a sweet smile I hadn't seen on his face until now.

"I'll try and be on my best behavior for you, girl," Aspen

mutters. He gives me the biggest grin before he jumps up onto my bed—shoes and all.

That will not work for me. Not at all.

"Will you get off?" I ask, attempting for *polite* as I stare at his shoes against the white comforter.

Aspen doesn't get off, though. Instead, he puts his hands behind his head and makes himself even more comfortable.

I repeat myself one more time—*another* time he decides not to listen.

I give him a few more seconds to respond appropriately before I slip one of my heels off. I raise it and smack Aspen in the arm with it. "Off my bed. *Now*."

It takes one more hit on his arm, and a shriek from Aspen that is *very* high-pitched, to remove him from my bed.

"Jesus, Veronica!" Aspen howls, rubbing the red spot my heel left on his arm.

Selma tucks her head into Maverick's neck, her body shaking with visible laughter. I even hear Maverick chuckle against her hair.

"You were on my bed. With shoes!" I reply in disgust. My hand sweeps the comforter clean where his dirty feet had been.

Aspen continues to rub the spot on his arm like I just impaled him with the heel. For someone whose muscles look like they belong in an Abercrombie and Fitch catalog, he's acting like a child.

My now-bare toes touch the tips of his tennis shoes and I look him right in the eye as I slowly say, "Just please don't get on my bed. M'kay?" I slowly pull a piece of lint off his T-shirt, my eyelashes batting at him as my lips pull into a smile.

"Got it," Aspen says under his breath at the same time he examines my body.

"Great, now can someone help me get the rest of my things?" I ask.

Maverick gives Selma a peck on the cheek before he retreats out of my bedroom door. Aspen follows close on his heels, but he takes a moment to look over his shoulder and wink at me before he disappears.

"Oh god," Selma groans, covering her face with her hand. "Lily is going to be pissed."

Part of me wants to ask her what she's talking about, but the bigger part of me doesn't care. Because when I look around my new room, I'm just happy to be away from Beaufort, South Carolina—where my parents live, and where my past still haunts me. Even though I'm definitely not fully separated from *living off Mommy and Daddy*, I'm a hell of a lot more independent than I was three months ago when I finally had the courage to leave.

Am I used to living in places three times nicer than this?

Yes.

But is this exactly where I feel like I need to be?

Also yes.

My past can't find me here—that I'm sure of.

"So, when do you want to fully move in?" Selma asks, bringing my attention back to her.

The more I look at her, the more I realize how beautiful she is. All of her features are soft, sincerity embedded in all of them. She wears her coppery brown hair short, so short it barely touches her shoulders. Her eyes are almond-shaped and lift at the corners. Though I'm probably most envious of her eyebrows. Where I have thinner, more arched eyebrows, hers are thick—every girl's eyebrow wet dream.

Bitch.

"Tomorrow?" I offer.

6

MAVERICK

I STARE at the droplet of condensation that slides down my beer. It slowly descends over the red label, slithers down the brown bottle, and disappears as it hits the old wooden tabletop of our booth.

"I can't believe we'll be gone for Thanksgiving," Lily rants from across the booth, taking a long pull of her own beer.

My twin sister Lily, Selma, and I sit at Lenny's. It's been a few hours since we showed Veronica the new place, and because we all have the night off, we met here for a few beers. Plus, it's been a few days since I've seen my sister, which I know drives her nuts. So here I am, being brother of the year.

"I know. I was looking forward to seeing your parents," Selma responds next to me, fumbling with the wrapper of her straw. She folds it over and over again.

"Oh, you'll still see them," Lily continues, resting her head on her hand and leaning closer to the two of us.

It's a Thursday night at Lenny's, which means it's packed with both underage and of age college students—it being Thirsty Thursday and all. The verdict is still out if this place will wind up getting shut down by the health inspector or the cops, but it's still one of my favorite places. It's familiar, an old hangout we've been coming to ever since we were all bright-eyed and eighteen and would do anything for a cheap beer we could get our hands on.

The walls of Lenny's are completely covered in dollar bills. Some of them are signed, or have pictures drawn on them. It's a typical dive bar. Old neon signs illuminate the place. Every table is covered in people's artwork and names.

"Did you hear that, Mav?" Lily questions, kicking me under the table.

"Hmm?" I ask, bringing my attention back to her. My hand absentmindedly finds Selma's leg next to mine, and I rest it against her thigh.

"Mom and Dad are coming to watch our tournament in Missouri over Thanksgiving holiday. They're staying in the same hotel as we are. The team is doing some fancy dinner for Thanksgiving. Which means you'll be all alone here. Unless you can come, too?"

Selma leans in closer to me, using her actions to show me she would also like me to be there to watch their volleyball tournament. Both of them play on the team, and they have a great chance of going to state this year. I wish I could be there to watch them.

"You know I can't," I begin, taking a moment to take a long sip of my beer. "I finally have the opportunity to shadow Keith Yang, and I can't let that opportunity go to waste." Keith Yang is not only my idol, he's one of the best criminal defense lawyers in our state. He's known to do pro bono cases all the time. I want to help people who've been wrongfully convicted of crimes and working with him is my first step in doing so. I hope to work at his firm when I complete law school. This is my chance at an *in* with him.

"Chug! Chug! Chug!" is chanted from across the bar. A group of frat guys cheer on one of their brothers as he chugs Lenny's famous pitcher—a concoction pertaining all the different beers that Lenny's serves. Everyone in our group has done the challenge at least once. Foam spills out from the sides of the guy's mouth as he chugs, but after a while he sucks it all down.

Selma's hand lands on mine, which is still in her lap. "We

wouldn't want you to miss this opportunity, Mav. We'll have plenty of other tournaments you can come to. I'm just sad you'll be spending Thanksgiving alone."

"I can check with Aspen to see what his plans are," I offer.

Lily makes a gagging noise from across the table. "Probably drowning in any chick he can get his grubby little hands on." She rolls her eyes and chugs the rest of her beer. It makes a clanking noise when she drops it back on the table. "Another!" she shouts, looking at Lenny at the bar, and asking for a fresh one like she's in Game of Thrones. "Seriously, Maverick, how are you even friends with that douche canoe?" Lily asks, peeling the wrapper off her beer bottle.

Screams erupt from another part of the bar, but this time none of us even glance that way. It's a typical noise here. We're so lost in our conversation that none of us even notice when Aspen walks up to us.

"Aww, Lily Bear, why do you have to be so sweet?" he asks, sliding in next to Lily and pulling her close to him. He pats the top of her head like he would a little sister, and through her grumbles, she shoves him.

"Gross, Aspen! Get your nasty hands off of me! Who knows where they have been recently." She fiercely rubs where he just touched her, being as overdramatic as usual when it comes to him.

Lenny comes to our table and sets a new beer down near the edge. Before Lily has a chance to take it, Aspen picks it up and chugs it in two seconds flat. Lily's look rivals the same one Veronica had when she was staring down that piece of paper.

If looks could kill, my best friend would very much be dead.

"Oh, stop being so dramatic, Lil," Aspen says, wiping his mouth with the back of his hand and setting it back on the drawn-all-over table. He makes eye contact with Lenny at the bar and holds up three fingers, putting his hand down when Lenny nods back at him. "Plus, I'm as clean as a whistle, baby." He grins at her and she rolls her eyes, scooting away from him in the booth.

I wonder if my sister realizes it's blatantly clear to both Selma and I that there's something more than *hate* between her and Aspen. There has been for the almost-four years we've been at college—but I'm certainly not going to be the first one to bring it up to either one of them. I just mind my own business in that regard.

"Did you tell your sister about my soulmate?" Aspen asks, looking over at Lily and waiting for her reaction.

I can tell he's trying to rile her up and get another reaction, which is exactly what he gets.

"Soulmate?" Lily sputters, wringing her hands together on top of the table.

"Yes, my soulmate is moving in with me. Things are getting serious," Aspen replies.

Lenny walks over and deposits three beers in front of Aspen, who hands one to me and the other to Lily. She begrudgingly takes it from him.

I finish off the last bit of my first beer before pushing it out of the way and setting the new one directly in front of me.

Selma must do something to Aspen underneath the table, because he jumps, giving her a scowl.

"He's lying," Selma starts, looking at Lily's pouting face earnestly. "Maverick found someone to pick up Kira's portion of the rent and move in with us. Aspen—for some reason—is under the impression that he and this girl, Veronica, are star-crossed lovers, but once you meet her you will *very* clearly see that she's not interested in him."

Aspen's hand flies to his chest in a mocking display. "You wound me, sweet Selma. Every woman is impressed by me."

"Not this one," Lily mutters under her breath, taking a long drink of her beer.

"*Especially* you, Lily Bear," Aspen says, tapping her on the nose with the tip of his finger.

Lily's eyes widen, and I can see her turning a new shade of pink.

These two, I swear.

My mind travels to Veronica for a split second, wondering where she is tonight. I hadn't thought to invite her out with us tonight, and now I'm wondering if I should have.

"Tell me about this *Veronica*," Lily says, dragging out her name with disdain.

I can't help but chuckle, which earns me a very dirty look from my twin sister.

A girl walks up to Aspen and tries to put her hand on him, but surprisingly, he waves her off and stays engaged in our conversation. Dismissed, the girl retreats to her large group of friends. They seem to console her, then send her in another man's direction twenty seconds later.

"Do you have anything to add, brother?" Lily asks, sitting back in the booth and crossing her arms over her chest.

There's a large rip in the red vinyl next to her, and I focus on that for a moment. I shake my head, wondering how it'll go between Veronica and Lily. I know there's a possibility the two of them could be friends—if that's something Veronica even has. All I know for certain is that Veronica wants nothing to do with Aspen, and therefore, there's nothing Lily needs to be jealous of when it comes to her.

Selma still sits quietly to the left of me, taking in the conversation. I lift my hand from her thigh and put my arm around her. I pull her in closer next to me, kissing her on the top of her curly hair.

"I'll tell you about her," Aspen says, looking over at Lily. "She reminds me of an ice queen. Her hair is so blonde, and it takes up half her body. She's filled with venom and ice. She even did this to me." He lifts the sleeve of his sweatshirt to show a forming bruise.

Dang, she actually did get him good.

"Keep going," Lily instructs, leaning in closer to Aspen, holding on to every word.

"I think she might hate me, but that's okay, I'll defrost her," Aspen says.

I can see where Aspen gets the ice queen reference for Veronica. At first glance she *is* all stone and ice, seemingly content in keeping everyone away from her. I wonder if she's always been so cold to people, or if something made her like this. Either way, it's not my concern, as long as she pays her rent.

"Maybe take the hint," Lily retorts, letting out a huff I can hear even in the loud bar.

"Never," Aspen responds. "I am going to figure the ice queen out." There's determination in his voice.

"Good luck with that," I scoff, stretching my legs out underneath the table.

"What's that supposed to mean?" Aspen asks.

"It means that girl has walls built so high it'll be impossible to climb them. Even for someone as persistent as you," I tell him.

"You say that like it's bad to build walls," my best friend responds, sitting taller in the booth.

Aspen would *decide to become philosophical when it comes to* her.

I open my mouth to respond, but Aspen adds, "Look, we don't know her story so before you go and write her off as some bitch, maybe consider there's more to it. Maybe she's just hard to get to know."

My mouth hangs agape as my best friend glares at me from across the table. I want to ask him if we're talking about the same girl—because I have a distinct memory of her thwarting him with a shoe only *hours* ago. I keep my words in, however, because his catch me off guard. I hadn't given much thought to why she acts the way she does—and I'm not going to start now.

"Can't wait to meet her," Lily quips in a dull tone.

I stifle the urge to tell my sister she's not missing much.

7

VERONICA

"Jesus Christ, Veronica," Aspen wheezes as he sets my last box of belongings next to my bed. "How the hell are you going to fit all that shit into this tiny room?" He looks around the room, where boxes are scattered all over, making it hard to walk anywhere.

I shrug and say, "Simple. I'll make it fit." The box cutter makes a ripping noise as it cuts through the tape on the box I open. When I lift the two flaps, I find it's my last box of shoes. One by one, I pull them out and walk them to the closet.

Aspen's right; it will be a tight squeeze, but I'll make it work. Everything I brought with me is a necessity—at least to me.

From the closet, I can hear Aspen's cell phone ring. He answers, engaging in a quick conversation with the person on the other end before hanging up. As I continue to neatly line my shoes on the closet shelf, Aspen fills the doorway.

"That was Selma," he says. "Someone called out of work today and they're short a waiter. I told her I'd come in, but I need to head out in ten minutes. You good in here?" His eyes catch on my sheer body suits hanging in the closet.

I give him a light shove on the shoulder. "Don't get any ideas, playboy. And I'll be fine here. I don't want anyone else unpacking my things anyway."

Aspen's gaze roams over my face, before he nods and leaves me to the peace and quiet of my new room.

Finally, I'm alone.

Even though I hate to admit it, Aspen is kind of growing on me. I don't want to send him any mixed signals on what he and I could be, though. He seems like a guy that could get attached very easily—and I don't do attachments.

Not anymore.

Not ever again.

I shake my head, trying to not let my mind wander in the direction it wants to go. It's already a drag being stuck in my head twenty-four/seven. All I do is hate myself. If anyone were to look into my thoughts, they'd find way too much self-loathing for a twenty-one-year old to have.

After the heels on my shelf are perfectly aligned, I step out of the closet and continue rifling through my things. The next box I open houses more clothes, which is great except I can't remember where Aspen put the box with all my hangers.

I look around my room, trying to find it. I zone in on the pile of boxes—almost as high as the ceiling—stacked against the wall by the window. A long sigh escapes me. Even though Aspen is easily six feet tall, my five foot seven is not near enough of a match to reach the boxes on the top.

Just as I consider moving on to a different task, footsteps sound from the stairs. Both Selma and Aspen are at work for the next five hours, which tells me the person coming down the stairs has to be Maverick.

He knocks on the trim of my door and says, "How's it going in here?"

Speak of the devil.

I turn around and take in his appearance—a black hoodie with navy blue basketball shorts. His cheeks are tinted pink from the cold front we're having in October here in Kansas. The dark strands of his hair fall over his forehead lazily and without effort.

"It's going fine," I say, "except I need hangers and I'm *pretty* sure they're in the box on top of this stupidly high pile Aspen created." I point to the stack of boxes going up the wall.

Since I stand directly in front of them, I'm sure Maverick can obviously pinpoint my dilemma. Even if I stand on my tiptoes with my arms outstretched, it would be nearly impossible to pull the box down without causing them all to tumble.

"I swear he did it on purpose so I would ask him to come back and help me," I grumble, twisting my hair from my ponytail around my finger. My bottom lip is caught between my teeth as I ponder what way I will torture Aspen for this later.

Maverick laughs as he crosses the distance to my side of the room. His shoulder brushes mine as he lands next to me, looking up at the pile Aspen created. "Aspen definitely did this to be able to have an excuse to come back in here." His long arms reach up and easily pull the box from the top. He sets it on the top of my bed before going back for the next one.

With those two boxes down, I can easily reach the rest of the stack. "Thank you," I mutter. I take the box cutter and open both boxes, pleased to see one of them in fact holds the hangers I need. Dropping the other box on the ground, I climb onto my bed and pour the hangers out, throwing the empty box in my discarded pile of other empty boxes.

As I begin to hang all my clothes on the hangers and start a pile of them, Maverick grabs the box cutter and starts breaking down the boxes. We work in a comfortable silence—and it weirds me out. I'm not used to men who are this comfortable in silence. Usually, they try to fill it, and unfortunately, it's normally with things they think I want to hear. But in the little time I've spent with Maverick, I'm starting to realize he isn't like most men. He's calmer, like he's at peace with himself.

He seems grounded. Maybe it's due to the fact that he's in a relationship that is *obviously* perfect. I've only been living with him and Selma for three days now, but in those three days I would have to be blind to see they weren't perfect for each other. They seem like best friends that happen to also be dating. I often found myself watching them, interested in their dynamic. I'd never witnessed two people so perfectly *in tune* with each other. Selma often finishes Maverick's sentences, and he's able to read her like a book, usually without her uttering a single word.

I'm envious of her, but not in the way people would expect.

Anyone could look at her and know she's a bright light. That she's *good* for him. I'm the opposite. Any man I decide to love is destined to drown with me in darkness. I'll never be the kind of girl who can pull a man from darkness. I'm the kind that pulls them into the depths with me, watching as they suffer.

My love is poison, and I'll never give it away again.

"How did you and Selma meet?" I ask Maverick, my curiosity getting the better of me.

His arm stops mid-cut through the box, his body tensing for a brief moment before it relaxes again. His blue gaze finds mine, and there is shock there. He probably sees the same shock in mine. I'm not normally one to get personal with people.

"Selma and I have been dating since high school. Our families have been very close for a very long time," he states.

The sound of tape being ripped fills the small room. His arms work quickly to break down the box and then he throws it out into the living area with the others he's already completed.

"We've known each other for basically as long as I can remember," he continues. "Selma's parents and my own have been planning our wedding since we first met when we were kids. We fought it for a long time, both perfectly content with being best friends. Then, things changed."

He shrugs and rolls the arm of his sleeve up, and I stop what I'm doing to watch him bend down to pick up another box. Except there are no more boxes to break down. His eyes stare at the boxes in the other room for a moment, his hands resting on his hips. A long breath escapes his lips.

"Things just…changed?" I ask quietly, still staring at him. I'm so enthralled in their love story, I don't even care if my question is invasive.

A hand runs against the buzzed sides of his hair as he nods. "Yeah." He pauses, his eyes wandering over the room. "Feelings got involved, among other things, and we've been together ever since."

Maverick takes the few steps to my bed and I curiously watch him climb onto it, where he pulls his long legs in to sit cross-legged across from me.

"What do you mean *among other things*?" I reach for a hanger at the same time the heater kicks on. The sound of the air flow is the only sound in the room as he thinks over his response to my blatant intrusion into his life.

"Look," he says.

His blue gaze pins me to my spot. My hands freeze as I stop halfway through putting a red blouse on a hanger.

He continues to stare at me with his next words. "I haven't asked into your personal life, so let's not get into mine. The spark notes version of my relationship with Selma is that we were friends that turned into something more. And now, we continue to navigate that something more." His eyes bore into mine for a moment longer before he picks up a hanger of his own and begins to hang one of my jean jackets on it.

"Well, you two seem perfect for each other. Happy," I say, my hands finishing their job of hanging the blouse. We both place newly-hung clothing in the growing pile.

"I love her," he states, making sure my eyes look at him before he starts his next task.

For some reason, his words make my stomach roll. I'm not sure why I feel those words all the way down to my core, but I do—and I have to get us to a new topic. I know I'm not jealous that *he* loves her.

I think I'm just slightly jealous that she's somebody worthy of love.

"So, tell me about this twin sister of yours," I say, successfully changing the subject.

He laughs, releasing a long sigh.

I sit there, continuing my task of hanging clothes, as his eyes rest on me. I can feel them examining my face, and I definitely feel them as they make their way down. They finally stop to rest on my hands as I work to hang the sweater.

"My twin sister is the complete opposite of me," he says. "I like to be a wallflower, take in my surroundings. She likes the attention to be fully on her. Where I'm calm, she is every bit of wild."

It's my turn now to stare at his hands. Since the sleeves of his hoodie are still rolled up, the muscles in his arm feather as he hangs one article of clothing after the other. I can't remember the last time I spoke to a man who wanted nothing from me. My body, my passion, my desire.

"I like her already." A smile breaks on my face, one that is genuine.

Maverick shakes his head, a smile forming on his face as well. "You two will be a match made in heaven. Or maybe it's hell. I'm actually kind of worried for the rest of us when the two of you strike up a friendship."

The sound of the heater turns off once again, leaving it almost completely silent in the room. Occasionally, there's the sound of a hanger bumping against another, but other than that, it's so *quiet*.

My mind wanders to the few friends I have. After thinking for a moment, I realize I don't really have any friends anymore. At one point in my life, I had many. Everyone wanted to be my friend. At least that's how it felt. But that time is in the past, and now I'd rather be without them. Without friends. Without anyone close.

Or so I thought. The more I get to know Maverick, and the more I hear about his twin, the more I realize I might like to be friends with the Morrison twins.

I'm content in the silence, lost in my own thoughts, but the tenor of Maverick's voice calls me back to where we are.

"My parents always say that when we were little, they were completely convinced one of us was switched at birth because we were so opposite," he says. "I never cried, and according to them, I essentially raised myself, whereas Lily needed supervision at all times. She constantly wanted to be held and would scream all night until someone picked her up. Lily still has that set of lungs on her, too. You should hear her when she and Aspen get in their classic arguments. I'm convinced people can hear them all the way on campus when they really get going."

The pile of clothes ready to hang has grown so big I'm afraid if we set anything else on top of it, it will go toppling down. I crawl off the bed and start to arrange the clothes in my hand so I can hang them in the closet.

"Why do they yell at each other?" I ask from inside my closet.

"Because they're basically the same person in two different bodies who happen to be attracted to each other."

I jump when Maverick's voice comes from the doorway. I was so distracted hanging my clothes in the appropriate spots that I didn't realize he'd gotten off the bed. Now, he's holding the rest of my clothes for me to hang.

"Wait a minute. Aspen has a thing for your sister?" I gawk. "And *she* has a thing for *him*?" I take the next piece of clothing from his hands and hang it with the rest of my T-shirts.

He laughs. "Well, yes and no. Neither one of them will admit it, but anyone in the same state as them can feel the chemistry burning. I'm not sure either one of them will do anything about it, though. They're both too content with hating each other to realize they like each other."

My mind turns this new information around. I have a feeling I'd like Lily based on Maverick's description of her, but I find it ludicrous she could be attracted to somebody like *Aspen*. To each their own, I guess.

As I take the last few pieces of clothing from Maverick's hand, his phone vibrates from the pocket of his sweatshirt.

He pulls it out, his eyebrows pulling together as he reads whatever's on the screen. He shoves it back into his pocket and looks at me. "I've got to take this."

I nod. We both stand across from each other awkwardly. "I'll see you later, Maverick."

He quietly mumbles a goodbye and leaves the room.

As his footsteps sound over my head, I finish hanging the rest of my clothes. It sounds like he's pacing up there, but I can't be sure. All I know is he continues to walk around for twenty more minutes as I finish unpacking for the night.

Finally, a door slams, letting me know he left.

Now, alone in the house—and alone in my head—my mind wanders to times I have no business reminiscing on.

8

VERONICA
FOUR YEARS AGO

THE GYMNASIUM WALLS of East Point High School reverberate from the sounds of the speakers. Homecoming has the gym packed with sweaty adolescents. I try to maneuver my way around a group of senior girls dancing to Usher and singing horribly off-key at the top of their lungs.

"Veronica! Wait up," my friend Daisy yells from a few yards away.

I feel my eyes roll in my head. I just wanted a moment of peace away from my meat-head date—and Daisy isn't exactly my definition of peace.

Her nasally voice falls in line right next to me. "Where's Jeff?" She looks around the gym to try to spot my date.

Daisy has always had a thing for Jeff, and she didn't talk to me for a week when he asked me to the dance instead of her.

"Probably in a circle jerk with his football friends," I retort, laughing at the mental picture.

Jeff is a nice guy—kind of. When he stops talking about himself for more than two seconds, that is. I can't blame him really. I'm not sure there's very much room left in his brain for intelligence judging by how huge his ego is.

Daisy raises her perfectly plucked eyebrows, her eyes going wide at the same mental picture. "Gross."

I reach a quiet corner of the gym after that, finally able to take a deep breath that doesn't smell like bodily odor or cheap perfume. "Go dance with him, Daisy," I say, not bothering to hide my annoyance with her.

"W-what?" she stutters out.

She fumbles with the rose of her corsage—a yellow one that goes with her sleek black dress.

"I said *you can go dance with him*," I repeat, getting more frustrated by the second.

"But he asked *you?*" Daisy looks at me with a face filled with confusion.

I can't help but think that maybe she and Jeff would be perfect together. Their conversations definitely wouldn't be of the deep matter, that's for sure. "Yes, he asked me, but you like him. So, go dance with him. I'm not into him anyway."

Daisy's pretty face breaks out into a huge grin that showcases her almost-perfectly-straight teeth. Her thin arms wrap around me in an embrace before she begins to shout in my ear. "You're the best, Veronica!" And then her brown hair bounces with her hasty steps back to the dance floor.

I take a long inhale in, finally happy in solace for the first time tonight. It's not that I'm not into school dances or anything. I'm a sixteen-year-old girl; dances are what we live for. But after grinding against Jeff's very noticeable hard-on for the last hour, I needed a break. It became way too tiresome to direct his sweaty hands away from going up my skirt.

"You're the best, Veronica!" a high-pitched—and very sarcastic—voice says behind me.

I turn around to see a guy leaning up against the bleachers. It's dark where he stands, and I can't quite make out his features to determine who he is. "Excuse me?" I ask, taking a step closer to the darkness.

"I find it so funny that you're so worshiped by your pretty little group of airheads that one seriously thanks *you* for allowing her to dance with a guy she's so obviously been obsessed with since freshman year," he explains.

The DJ switches to a cheesy slow song, making the gymnasium not quite as loud as before. I step closer to the voice and come face-to-face with the rude asshole who's apparently hell bent on insulting me tonight.

I wish I recognized him. East Point is a fairly large high school, and I admit I don't quite take my time remembering every face that attends here.

"She was being polite. He was *my* date after all," I snarkily respond, trying hard not to notice that no matter how big of an asshole this guy is, he's kind of cute.

He's wearing a pair of black dress pants—like every other guy in the gym—but instead of the cookie-cutter white button-up shirt and tie, he has on a pastel-printed argyle shirt with a pink bowtie. And he's pulling it off nicely.

He throws his head back in a laugh, exposing his strong throat and Adam's apple. "Oh my god," he says. "You really thought you were doing the whole world a favor by letting her dance with him, didn't you?" His hands run down his face with his laughter, pulling at his cheeks and making them appear larger.

I pull my face into a scowl. I really don't know what he's trying to hint at here. Jeff is my date. Of course Daisy should have asked before she went and grinded her ass against his Netherland.

"And who are you again?" I ask him, my hand finding my hip as I glare at him.

When he finally answers, he says, "Of course you don't know who I am. Why would East Point's princess know anybody that isn't in her royal posse?"

My jaw falls open. I don't know what I've ever done to this guy to warrant the third degree he's currently giving me. My heart beats faster in my chest as adrenaline pumps through my veins. If I didn't fear the unnecessary attention from others—the bad kind of attention—I probably would have slapped this guy already.

Normally I don't stop to care what people think of me, but for some reason it irks me that this stranger has such a low opinion of me.

"Look, I'm sorry if this damages the obviously large ego you have, but no, I don't know your name. If you tell me it, maybe we can get past whatever grudge you have toward me," I say, absentmindedly spinning one of my long blonde curls around my finger in nervous habit.

He narrows his eyes at me, obviously considering his next move. "Connor Liams."

I extend my hand out to him, my thick stack of bracelets jingling with the motion. "Nice to meet you, Connor Liams. I'm Veronica Cunningham."

The corner of his lip lifts in a hint of a smile. The longer I look at him, the more I realize he is really cute. A mop of curly, dirty blond hair sits at the top of his head. It's hardly tamed, and it looks like parts of it might even still be wet, like he just quickly showered and threw on whatever he could find for homecoming. I notice a boutonniere pinned to his chest, reminding me of the fact that he must have arrived with a date.

I wonder where she is, but I don't ask.

"I know who you are," he says, his green eyes crinkling at the corner with a smile.

"Well, I don't know who you are," I reply as the DJ switches back to an upbeat song. I take a step closer to him, knowing whatever his next words will be that it'll be harder to hear him over the sounds of the DJ.

"And I guarantee you won't spend the time to get to know me," he bluntly says.

I don't like being told what to do, and I don't take well to people telling me about myself. "Try me."

His cheeks spread in a wide smile as he pushes himself off the bleachers. He finally extends a hand toward me, and I don't hesitate to take it. His large hand engulfs mine; it's warm and even a bit sweaty—but for some reason, it feels right.

So, I let the complete stranger—who obviously isn't my biggest fan—lead me out of the crowded high school homecoming, unknowing where we'd end up next.

9

VERONICA

THE SOUND of feet stomping above my head wakes me from the vivid memory in my dream. Something hard digs into my stomach and when I roll over, I realize it's one of the hangers from the night before. I must have fallen asleep after Maverick left. I let my eyes drift closed once more when the sound of stomping once again shakes the ceiling of my basement bedroom.

"Ugh!" I grumble against my silk pillowcase. I'm fairly confident I could kill Aspen I'm so angry.

Selma is too skinny to be making that much noise and Maverick moves with too much grace. That only leaves my dear friend Aspen. And he is suddenly very high on my shit list.

Rolling over, I rub my eyes, trying to clear my head from the dream I was having. A nightmare, really, now that it's over. In it, I was still with Connor. And I'm struck with the harsh reality that he's not here with me.

I rarely let my mind wander to my high school days. There's nothing for me to remember from that time of my life other than pain and devastation. When I let my mind wander to those days after Maverick left last night, it sent me into a spiral of memories. The recollections following me even after I finally closed my eyes—hoping to escape them.

I'm just starting to get out of bed when a knock sounds at

my door. I didn't even hear anyone come down the stairs, but I get up to open it regardless.

"Aspen, I might full on throttle you for waking me up," I say, opening the door expecting to find Aspen on the other side, but instead there's a grinning Maverick.

"Oh, Veronica." He sighs. "Please don't ever say that to Aspen as a threat. He will view that as more of a prize."

"Shit. You're right." I leave the door open and walk back into my room, not worried if Maverick is coming in or not.

Walking over to my mirror, I remember I am still in my pajamas. I look down at them before looking back up at Maverick. "Mind waiting out there for a minute? I need to change." He nods, walking out the door he just came in.

"Aren't you going to be late for class?" His voice echoes from the other side of the wall.

I quickly undress, putting on a fresh bra and new underwear. I reach for the first articles of clothing I can find. When I'm fully dressed, I peek out into the common area of the basement. I find him staring at the black TV screen, his hands shoved into the pockets of his tan chinos and his backpack slung lazily over one of his shoulders.

"Maybe," I respond to his question from earlier.

I roll my eyes as the stomping above our heads persists. It sounds like an elephant is up there. Honestly, it's impressive somebody with that toned of a body type can make this much noise.

"I happen to be in the same class as you and I can confirm we are about to be very late if you don't get ready right this moment," Maverick says.

I roll my eyes. I'm late to this class every time I have it, but I don't have to point that out to him. I grab a pair of socks from a basket on the shelf and slip them on my feet, a pair of tennis shoes following after.

My hands are pulling my hair into a messy bun when he steps back into my room.

I check my phone as I pull it off the charger and throw it into my purse. The belongings in my purse rustle around as I open it to double check that my laptop is still in there. I guess if

Maverick's going to make me attend class, I should at least bring what I need.

"How long did it take you to realize we shared a class?" I ask, sidestepping him to get out of my room. The lecture hall we're in fits up to two-hundred people, making it easy to forget all the faces. I hadn't known we were in the same class, but it's not like I ever try to notice anyone. I spend most of the lectures doodling in my notebook, not bothering to pay attention to my surroundings. Our arms brush as I make my way to the basement bathroom.

I let out a long breath as I take in my appearance. I'd prefer to put makeup on before leaving, but I'm vain enough to know I don't need it. I do have a sleep indentation on my face from something I fell asleep on, though. The sound of running water fills the bathroom as I hold my toothbrush underneath it.

Maverick appears in the doorway. "I noticed you during the first class. It was kind of hard to miss the fact that somebody was fifteen minutes late on the first day."

I smile even though my toothbrush is in my mouth. "It was syllabus week," I retort, but it sounds jumbled because I have a mouthful of toothpaste and spit.

His wet hair flops around as he shakes his head, laughing. "I thought our professor was gonna have a heart attack when you said that to his face. I've never seen that shade of red on a human being before."

I spit out the toothpaste and use the cup next to the sink to rinse out the rest of my mouth. My eyes sadly look at my skin-care products so neatly laid out on the counter. I don't have time to do my whole regimen this morning if we're going to get to class on time.

"Well god forbid I do that again. Let's go then." I gesture for him to lead the way, but he doesn't budge. "Can I help you?" I ask, adjusting my purse on my shoulder.

He watches me for a moment longer, his eyes narrowing on me like he's trying to figure something out. "I just thought you'd put up more of a fight."

I laugh, shaking my head at him as I head toward the stairs.

I feel my messy bun bounce on the top of my head as I run up the stairs.

When I look over my shoulder, I find Maverick climbing them behind me, a puzzled look still on his face. I fight the urge to laugh again. I didn't put up a fight because I'd planned to actually attend class today.

He doesn't have to know that, before I accidentally fell asleep, I had every intention of setting an alarm for class.

10

VERONICA

"WHAT IN THE hell did we just listen to?" I ask Maverick as we walk out of our sociology class. We spent a majority of the lecture listening to our middle-aged professor talk about the My Little Pony conference he went to over the weekend. I'm not kidding. He was telling us how he was a proud *brony*—AKA a bro who loves My Little Pony.

Maverick chuckles, raising his hand to wave at someone across the building who just shouted his name. "I have no idea. I think I stopped listening when he started listing his favorite ponies."

We stop to wait for a group of people leaving the large lecture hall.

"At least you made it that far. He lost my attention the second he hopped on his soap box to discuss the importance of grown men loving fictional ponies," I say.

Maverick holds the door open for me as we make it out into the crisp Kansas air. Admittedly, I love the fact that Kansas has actual seasons. Where I'm from in South Carolina, we basically go from hot to a little less hot. We're halfway through October, which means the trees here are starting to change colors as well. I wouldn't tell anyone this, but I kind of love it here.

We both stop in front of the building. I have a discussion

class I have to be at in fifteen minutes. On the days I do attend classes, I'm already halfway there by now.

"Well, I need to get to my next class," I explain, looking up at Maverick.

His eyes are on something over my shoulder, a smile spreading across his face. A perfect set of dimples forms on both of his cheeks, and for some reason, I want to reach out and poke them. When I turn around to see what he's smiling at, I find Selma and another girl walking toward us.

"Is there any way you could wait a minute, Veronica?" His ocean eyes find mine.

And even though I want to make it to my next discussion class early to get my spot in the corner where no one bothers me, I find myself planting my feet and waiting. "Sure," I say, kicking around some fallen leaves on the sidewalk with the toe of my sneakers.

My eyes wander to the two girls closing in on us. I stare as Maverick envelops Selma in a hug, his whole body smothering her. He places a loving kiss to her forehead before pulling the other girl in. Just when I think he might hug the other one, he puts his large hand on top of her head and squeezes. She proceeds to punch him in the arm, and then the puzzle pieces fall together for me.

This must be his twin sister. Lily.

"You're a pain in my ass," she huffs, glaring at Maverick who's too busy reaching for Selma's hand to pay her any notice.

Then, a pair of blue eyes that look just like Maverick's fall on me.

"Hi, I'm Lily, but you must already know that." She flips the long, dark, blanket of hair over her shoulder and smiles at me.

I smile.

I like her already.

"Veronica," I respond, taking a moment to take in her outfit of choice.

She's wearing a pair of jeans, a black T-shirt, and a pair of checkered Vans on her feet. A purse almost identical to my own is perched on one of her shoulders. Her dark hair—a few shades darker than Maverick's—falls all the way down past her boobs. I have the urge to ask her what products she uses because I can see how shiny her hair is, even from a few feet away.

But Lily looks over to Maverick and Selma; they're busy having a hushed conversation between themselves.

My Apple watch buzzes on my wrist, alerting me to a missed text. When I notice what time it is, I realize I need to be huffing it across campus if I'm going to make it to my discussion class on time.

"It was cool to meet you, Lily," I begin, backing away from our small group. "But I need to get to my next class."

Selma and Maverick seem too deep in conversation to even notice that I'm about to leave, but I do get a quick goodbye from Lily, with her telling me we'll talk later when she comes over.

The group is almost out of sight when Maverick yells across the quad, "Bye, Veronica! Save Princess Cupcake from My Little Pony for me!"

I roll my eyes and flip him the bird. I'm positive he just rattled off a bunch of random objects to create a fictional name, and now everyone within earshot thinks I'm just as obsessed with My Little Pony as our professor is.

11

VERONICA

A FEW HOURS after my last class, I'm sitting on my bed scrolling through Instagram. My favorite face mask is seeping into my pores when my bedroom door flies open. I'm two seconds from throwing my phone across the room and shouting Aspen's name when I realize he isn't the culprit.

No, this culprit is barely five feet tall and has the biggest grin on her face.

"Hi, Veronica!" Lily says, helping herself in as she looks around my room.

I sit there with my mouth wide open as she takes in her surroundings. Apparently, she likes what she sees because she closes the door behind her and waltzes right in.

As soon as I got home from my classes, I finished unpacking the rest of my stuff. It took me almost three hours, and I had barely rested for fifteen minutes before she came barging on in.

Out of instinct, I want to shove her tiny body right back out the door when she has the audacity to sit down on my white comforter in front of me. I've gotten so used to this knee-jerk reaction to people—whether I like them or not—it's now my norm.

"Can I help you?" I ask, not bothering to hide the irritation in my voice.

"Yes, you can, *actually*," Lily replies, pulling at a split end of her hair. She tosses the strand of hair back down and focuses on me. "Selma and Maverick are locked alone in their room, which is *gross*," she explains, "and Aspen is boring me to death since he's all caught up in his video game. So, I figured I'd come down here and get to know my new friend a little better."

"Who said we were friends?" If I didn't have a face mask on that hinders me from showing any emotion, my eyebrows would be raised all the way to my hairline.

I met this girl six hours ago and suddenly we're friends?

I want to laugh. I don't have very many friends, and I certainly don't make them that fast. If we were friends, she'd know that.

Lily sighs, but a smile pulls at the corners of her lips. "Oh, we *are* friends, Veronica. You'll find that it's easier to agree with me than to try to put up a fight."

I think about her response for a moment. There's a small part of me that perks up inside at the prospect of having a new friend. It's unwelcome, but it's there.

I've alienated myself from all the friends I grew up with, and I don't regret it for a second. It's an after effect of deciding you're done with attachments. An aftershock. But that doesn't mean that every now and then I don't wish I had someone to tell dumb things to, or maybe help me pick out jeans that don't make my ass look huge.

"We'll see." My response must satisfy her, because she drops the topic.

Instead of continuing to fill the silence, she hops off my bed and starts to take inventory of my room. She picks something up from my bedside table.

It's one of my pieces of art.

I used oil paints to portray the deep green eyes. Even though most people would focus on those, the reason I painted it in the first place was to showcase the eyebrows. Over the left eye sits a scar that runs completely through the honey brown eyebrow.

An imperfection.

I remember the first time I laid eyes on that imperfection. My hands had twitched at my sides, practically begging to grab a paintbrush to get to work.

"What is this?" she asks, staring at the piece a moment longer before carefully setting it back on the white nightstand.

I barely hear her, my mind too wrapped up in memories with the person that imperfection belonged to.

"Nothing," I respond, too tired and numb to tell her the story behind the painting.

Surprisingly, Lily lets me skirt away from her question. She continues her trek around my room, picking up random things as she goes. "Oh my god, you went to a True Minds concert?" She stares greedily at a pair of concert tickets I have tucked into a corner of my full-length mirror.

"Yep," I respond, touching the substance on my face to see if it's completely dry yet.

My face feels like I'm on my twentieth round of Botox, it's so numb. No matter how hard I try, I can't move any of my features. I realize I have to keep the gunk on my face, though. Because when I pull my finger away, I notice a hint of green on it, meaning it's still wet.

"I would literally give my left tit to go to one of their concerts!" she cries, her eyes going wide as she stares at me.

"It kind of sucked," I reply, going back to perusing my Instagram feed.

My fingers stop on a photo of someone from my past. If I was a nice human being, I would like it, maybe even leave a comment, but I don't. Instead, I stare at her for a moment longer before continuing to scroll.

When I look up from my phone, Lily is peering at me with a look of betrayal on her face, like she might be reconsidering her statement of us being friends.

"I'm going to pretend you didn't just say that," she whispers, carefully putting the tickets back in the corner of my mirror like they were the most fragile items on this Earth. "I literally begged my dad to fly me to one of their stadium shows so I could see them. Unfortunately, none were close enough for him to let me go alone."

"You didn't miss much." I throw the white comforter off me and retreat out of my room and into the basement bathroom. There, I turn on the water and leave my fingers under the sink to test its temperature. When it finally warms up—which takes way too long considering Lily is still snooping in my room—I wash the green gunk off my face. I'm just finishing up wiping all the water off my face when footsteps come barreling down the stairs.

I consider quickly slamming the door and hiding out in here to avoid the one person who makes that much noise in this house, but I decide I'm too interested in seeing the famous banter between Lily and Aspen.

"Veronica!" Aspen singsongs, blocking me from leaving the small bathroom.

"Ass hat," I sweetly sing back to him, ducking under his arm before he can capture me in there alone with him.

Lily walks out of my closet, with one of my black corset tops wrapped around her body and over her actual outfit. "How do you get into this thing?"

She's still fiddling with the ties that run all the way up when Aspen comes into my room and whistles.

"Damn, little sister," he begins. "What are you thinking putting that on? You wouldn't even be able to keep that thing on because your boobs are so small."

Just like Lily had done twenty minutes prior, Aspen comes in and sits his ass on my comforter like he owns the place.

What is up with these people thinking they can barge right in and sit on my bed?

I narrow my eyes at him, sending him a look that hopefully conveys—loud and clear—that if his feet touch my bed, I *will* get my heels out and beat him with them again.

Lily purses her full lips, her perfect eyebrows drawing together on her forehead. "Please, Aspen." Her hands go to grab her perky boobs underneath the corset. "Let's not pretend you don't fantasize about these puppies every time you jerk off." She jiggles them in her hands, and I watch with piqued interest as his eyes zone in on them.

This is going to be so *much fun to witness.*

A few moments later, Lily's back in my closet and Aspen is rubbing his eyes, muttering something under his breath.

"You okay there, bud?" I ask, leaning my hip against my dresser.

"Sure thing," he responds, continuing to rub his eyes like he just saw his grandmother naked. "Just trying to scrub that mental picture out of my brain. Absolutely disgusting."

I shake my head, damn well knowing he thought that little show was far from disgusting.

Lily comes out of the closet, a stack of clothes in her hands. "I'm going to borrow a few things from you, Veronica. Sound good?"

I want to argue with her, but I know I have way more clothes than I actually need.

Plus, if she takes a few things it gives me the excuse to go shopping for new clothes to replace them.

"Whatever." I grab my hairbrush from the dresser and run it through my hair.

I can see Lily and Aspen in the mirror. Because of that, I don't miss it when she sticks her tongue out at him. A few seconds later, he flips her the bird.

"What are you doing down here, Aspen?" I ask, trying to undo a tangle in my hair.

"I'm bored," he whines. "Let's have a game night!" His eyes light up at the idea.

My nose scrunches. I already planned my night around drinking the wine I bought after flirting with the guy at the liquor store. A game night with people is the last thing I want to do.

"There's only three of us," Lily points out, taking a seat next to him on my bed. She pulls her phone out of her jacket pocket and glances at it for a moment.

"Is that Bumble?" Aspen inquires, trying to peer over her shoulder.

Lily is too quick for him, her phone already shoved back into her pocket before he can sneak another glimpse. "Mind your own business!" She scoots as far away from him on the bed as her body will allow.

He rolls his eyes at her, stepping off the bed and going out into the main area.

We both watch curiously as he pulls blanket after blanket off the blanket ladder.

Just when I'm about to ask him what in the hell he's doing, he grabs the ladder on both sides and starts knocking the ceiling with it. "Maverick! Selma! Stop making out for two seconds and come have game night with us." He continues to obnoxiously pound the ceiling with the ladder, and little specks of white start to rain down on him.

Lily and I remain in my doorway. This goes on for two more minutes before we finally hear an echo of footsteps above us.

Aspen snickers, putting the blanket ladder back up against the wall. "Always does the trick," he mutters as both Selma and Maverick come into view.

12

MAVERICK

SELMA WAS asleep next to me in bed as I worked on a research paper when I heard the first *thud*. At first, I didn't pay it much attention. I figured Veronica was moving something around in her room, or maybe Aspen had a guest over, but after the thudding continued and woke Selma up, we decided to go check out what was going on. We were both climbing out of the gray cotton bed sheets when we heard Aspen shout at us about a game night.

"What do you think?" Selma had asked, stretching her arms to the ceiling. She rifled through our clean laundry basket and pulled on a pair of black leggings.

"I think if we don't go down there, he'll never stop yelling for us, which might aggravate Veronica enough to impale him with another one of her high heels," I said.

Selma laughed, then picked up her glasses from the nightstand and perched them on her nose.

Now, thirty minutes later, we're caught up in an Aspen game night. What I thought would just be the four of us that live here has turned into a gathering of eight people.

Lily was already here, which I was too holed up in my room to even realize, and then Aspen invited three more of his friends —Derrick, Tristan, and Beau. All of which play on our college baseball team, including Aspen.

We're crammed around our old card table, playing a game of Cards Against Humanity. In each round of the game, a winner is chosen, who becomes the next person to choose between all the cards.

The loser, so far, is Aspen's friend Derrick. The winner, by far, is Veronica. Turns out the ice queen has a sense of humor, because her cards keep getting picked as the funniest.

Lily is busy looking through the cards she's been given, trying to pick her favorite and her least favorite.

"Oh, hurry up, could you?" Aspen taunts from across the table.

"Shut up, Aspen," Lily responds, rifling through the cards even slower now that Aspen has commented on it.

"Take your time," Tristan says next to Veronica, earning himself a glare from Aspen.

Tristan just smirks at him and goes back to his conversation with Veronica. The two of them have their heads bent close together, and I observe them as she makes a show of flirting with him. My eyes flick to Aspen, who's still blatantly glaring at them.

"This one!" Lily says, slapping a card down on the table, the sound loud enough to cause Aspen's eyes to snap to her.

"That's mine again, losers," Veronica responds with a teasing smile, reaching across to take the card to put it in her winning pile.

The girl has a decent sized stack going. Certainly bigger than anyone else's.

"Oh, I meant that one was the loser," Lily responds, shrugging her shoulders at Veronica in apology.

My eyes narrow on Lily. I know for a fact she had chosen that one as winner before she decided to change her mind.

Lily picks through the cards she was given one more time before slapping a new one on the table. "Now this is the real winner. Ha ha, *sooo funny!*"

We all look at the card, in silence. It doesn't even make sense.

Everyone is still quiet when Derrick realizes his card actually won. He shoots up like a firecracker into the sky on the Fourth of July.

We all watch him with amusement because we know his card wasn't actually funny, but Lily gave him a break anyway.

"Does he really not understand that he just got a pity one?" Selma sweetly whispers into my ear.

She sits in a ball on my lap. Her arms wrap around her legs, and any time she moves I have to adjust underneath her to get comfortable again. Whenever she leans back, the short strands of her hair tickle my neck.

"I doubt it," I whisper in her ear. My gaze finds Veronica and Tristan at the same moment she busts out laughing. I don't think I've actually ever heard her laugh until now.

I'm curiously watching them interact, wondering what he could have said to get the stoic Veronica to react in such a way. Before now, I haven't seen anything but annoyance come from her.

"Maverick!" Lily shouts, snapping her tan fingers in my direction. I look up from the spot I was staring a hole into at the table and try to wipe the confusion off my face. Selma's body turns in my lap to look at me, giving me an inquisitive look.

"Are you going to play a card this round?" Lily questions.

13

VERONICA

I WATCH Maverick with fascination as he clearly tries to pull his thoughts together—about what, I have no idea. The whole table is silent, waiting for him to pick a card from his hand and play it. Lily waits impatiently, tapping her foot against the tattered rug below her.

"Oh yeah," Maverick says under his breath. He quickly sorts through the cards in his hands before throwing one down. He doesn't even look to see the card he's filling in the blank for.

Lily narrows her eyes at him from across the table, clearly aware *something* is off about him right now. She doesn't say anything, though her eyes find Aspen who's looking through the white cards to pick his favorite.

My eyes should be on Aspen as well, but they aren't. I'm too focused on watching Selma and Maverick in curiosity. She still sits in his lap, but her body now faces his. She has a puzzled look on her face just before she whispers something under her breath to him, but his only response is a shake of his head. He watches Aspen read through the cards he's been given.

It registers a few seconds late that the chosen winning card is the one I played.

I bend across the table. "That would be mine! Thank you, Aspen." I pluck my card out of his fingers and set it in my large pile.

My body falls back into the uncomfortable fold-up chair I've been sitting in for the past hour. I cross my legs and look at Tristan, who's currently staring at me.

He leans closer to me, moving my blonde hair from where it cascades down the front of me, so it rests down my back. His breath tickles me as he pulls his body close to mine, his lips almost touching my ear.

"Let's go," I say to Tristan, grabbing the wine bottle I've been drinking in one hand and Tristan's hand in the other. My door is only a few steps away. I lead him inside and refuse to look over my shoulder at the inquisitive gazes I still feel on my back.

As soon as the door shuts, Tristan's lips are on mine. They are hard and persistent, and it's the perfect combination to wipe everything else from my brain. His hands are calloused, probably from baseball, and I love the way they feel when they scratch against my skin.

I let him guide me to the bed, unashamed that I can still hear voices right outside the door.

The only thing I can think of right now is the way Tristan's lips travel across my body.

This.

This is the feeling I crave. The feeling I live for.

"You won't stay the night in here," I tell Tristan as he peels my leggings off.

"I won't stay the night in here," he repeats, his eyes hooked on the lower half of my body.

"This won't happen ever again." It comes out quickly, my body anticipating where his mouth will hit next. I tell this same thing to every guy I hook up with.

Because I can't give them any more than my body for a night.

And I don't want anything more than their body for a night.

I WAKE up the next morning, happy to find that Tristan kept up his end of the bargain. The other side of my bed is empty and cold—just like I prefer it.

Footsteps echo above my head, multiple sets of them. I am not in the mood to see anyone right now, so I turn over in my bed and grab my phone from the nightstand. When I look at it, I see that I have two missed calls from my mother. Why she feels the need to call me twice before ten a.m., I have no idea, but instead of dodging her calls all day, I swipe to call her back.

As the phone rings, I sit up in bed and pull my feet in. There's a loose thread coming out of my comforter, so I pull on it.

She finally picks up after four rings. "Veronica?" she asks hesitantly.

"Hi, Mother," I respond, still playing with the loose strand.

I can hear one of the barstools being pulled across the hardwood floors above me.

"Glad to see you could make time for your own mother. You must have one busy schedule," she says, and I don't miss the aggression in her voice.

My mother and I haven't always had a strained relationship. There was a time when we had constant spa dates together. We'd hit up our favorite boutiques afterward, with our fresh faces and nails, but that time has come to pass.

My mom hasn't changed at all—but I have.

I went from a sheltered, spoiled, selfish, but still decent daughter, to a fuck-up. A life ruiner. At this point, I'm not sure I know how to be anyone other than someone who lashes out at others—especially the people who know of every single one of my mistakes, and the lowest points of my life.

"I don't have classes on Fridays," I respond lazily, trying to keep the conversation from getting too deep.

Unfortunately, my mother knows me better than anybody. I know she can see through all my bitchy bullshit. But for some reason, she puts up with it. After a few years, she probably realized this is just who I am now.

"Will you be coming home for Thanksgiving?" she asks.

"I can't, Mom. I'm sorry." And I am sorry. Part of me

wishes I was stronger than I am, that I could go back to that town and face my past, but I can't—even if that means I can't face my own parents.

"Your father would really like to see you," she presses on, not willing to go down without a fight.

My mind races through excuses on why I can't make it. In reality, I have nothing happening here to prevent me from going home except my own cowardice. We have fall break coming up, which gives us the whole week of Thanksgiving off. Clementine had offered to give me that time off as well so I could go home and visit family, but I didn't take her up on it.

"I know." I pause, taking a deep breath. "I have to work that week. I can't take off." It's a lie I should feel guilty about, but I don't.

Nothing could weigh heavier on my conscience than what I've done in my past. Nothing could be more violent than the waves that ocean town brings back.

"You know you don't need that silly job, Veronica. We can more than afford to pay for your well-being while in college. Tell that eccentric boss of yours that you're coming home, or you'll quit," my mom says.

"I can't just quit, Mom. I need this job. It's my chance to get my paintings in a real gallery, maybe even get a buyer or two to buy some of them. I'll make it up to you and Dad, I promise."

"Sweetie, you know we could tell our friends at the club about your paintings. I'm sure you'd get some buyers that way," she offers.

I scoff. There's no way I want my name attached to any of my paintings, especially in front of the people back home. They're the *last* people I would allow to see inside the dark crevices of my soul should my paintings ever be put on display.

Nope.

I'd rather remain anonymous and make shit money at a gallery in exchange for the chance to have them hanging on the walls there.

The scratching of the barstools against the hardwood floor screeches again above me. Aspen is ranting about something before the sounds stop, and then there is nothing.

"The Liams have been asking about you." My mom pauses, waiting for a response from me.

Except, I have none.

I'm stuck in a moment that happened years ago. A moment that came and went. A moment that took most of me with it when it left.

My hands are clammy as they grip the phone. She just betrayed me. She knows not to bring them up. To never bring them up. It's a punch to my gut—no, to my throat—when I hear that name.

I don't even say goodbye. Like a child, I hang up the phone and throw it across my bed in an attempt to escape her and her meddling.

The phone makes a soft *thump* against my fluffy white comforter. I wish I could have thrown it down on hard concrete, shattering the phone in pieces. Anything to ensure my mother could never mutter that last name again.

No matter how hard I fight against them, the memories rush in—and I am paralyzed.

14

VERONICA
FOUR YEARS AGO

IT'S THREE A.M., and I've had one of the best nights of my life. After spending hours at a local arcade, Connor and I have ended up in a small diner outside of town.

"So, you're cooler than I thought," Connor says, taking a long pull from the straw to his milkshake.

I am fascinated by the way his cheeks pull together when he takes a drink, his lips working strongly against the straw.

"What's that supposed to mean?" I ask sarcastically, taking a drink of my own milkshake.

"I don't know," he mumbles. "You just seem...uptight all the time."

"Uptight?" My voice comes out in a screech, making my own ears cringe.

He laughs. "Yeah, very uptight. And well, you kind of come off as a bitch."

My mouth hangs open. I'll be the first to admit it, I'm not the nicest girl at East Point, but I didn't think I came off as a bitch to strangers.

His pink bowtie has been loosened around his neck, and the red lights of the diner reflect off his face. He stares at me, allowing me time to work through his comment in my head.

"I guess I don't really care what people think about me." I look away from him, staring down at my red dress. My mother and I had so much fun picking it out a month ago. It's made of a deep red satin material. The neckline plunges between my cleavage, or lack of cleavage. At the waist, it cinches in and then flares out in an A-line shape, making my already slim waist appear even slimmer.

"Is that just something girls say to appear tough, but deep down they really do care?" He dips a fry into his chocolate milkshake, and I crinkle my nose at the mix of flavors.

I shrug. "I don't let people get close enough to know the real me. If they don't know who I really am, then I don't care about their opinion of me."

The waitress comes over, asking us if we need anything. We both shake our head before she retreats back to the kitchen. The diner has an older couple on the side of the restaurant, along with an old man sitting alone a few booths down from us. Other than that, it's empty.

"But why wouldn't you just let people see that you might not be the huge bitch that they all think you are?" His face is full of confusion. I feel weird under his gaze.

I lather my tater-tot in ketchup, popping it into my mouth and slowly chewing. He watches me, waiting for a response. "Maybe I am a bitch."

His lips pull into the smile I'm quickly becoming a fan of. "Maybe," he retorts. "But somehow I think there's more to you than meets the eye."

My heart starts to race in my chest, and I want to flee this diner and get away from him. He can see me, see past my exterior I've built, and I don't like it. I'd rather keep everyone at arm's length. I'm a fan of shallow relationships, neither party delving too deep into the psyche of the other, but somehow, I think that Connor only keeps his relationships deep.

I shrug, trying to come off more nonchalant than I feel. "No one ever sticks around long enough to see."

I hesitantly watch the slow rise of his shoulders. He stares at me, his eyes slightly narrowing, and it feels like he can see every thought or feeling I've ever had.

"What if I want to?" His stare only becomes even more intense, which I didn't even know was possible. The diner is quiet, and it's quite possible that even from across the booth, he can hear my heart slamming against my chest.

I throw my blonde hair over my shoulder, trying to appear as nonchalant as possible. Putting up my shields that were just slightly lowered right back into place. I pull my lips into a smile, "You won't."

And then I reach across the table and steal one of his fries.

I CAN TASTE the chocolate of the milkshake on my tongue as if it were yesterday. I can feel the way his green eyes analyzed every last part of me. It's agonizing. My skin itches and much to my dismay, my eyes fill with tears.

It was the best night of my life.

It led to the best year of my life.

And then, it led to the worst times of my life—to the hell I'm still living in.

Connor and I were just friends for a week before his witty jokes and persistence won my heart. He was the silly boy in love with the entitled girl. We were never bound to work. But we were happy in our short-lived fairytale. He consumed every part of me. There wasn't a single part of me that didn't also belong to him. It turned out that my hard armor was guarding the softest heart. A heart that danced out of my chest and made a home in him in less than seven days.

A sob escapes me as our year together flashes through my head.

The soft curls of his hair. His dumb jokes. The way his body didn't fit into the coupe my parents gifted me on my birthday. The way he loved every inch of me. The way I loved being his. The way I loved *feeling* love.

The way I felt when it came to a crashing end.

It all flies through my head until I can't pinpoint what is my reality and what is my past. I hit my pillow with my balled fist over and over, trying to release the tension in my body, the tension in my mind.

I can hear my phone vibrating on the end of my bed—probably my mother.

I want to answer it and yell at her. To scream at her for uttering the name I never want to hear again, can't afford to hear again.

But I don't have it in me to battle her. I can't even battle my own demons right now, let alone her.

So I let the tears fall from my eyes until my naked skin dampens. My naked skin that is still naked from the night before with Tristan.

The irony crosses my mind. The fact that these tears I cry

for the boy who knew me inside and out are washing my naked, dirty body from a night with a guy I hardly know.

I think of Connor. He was constantly trying to make me better, trying to prove to me that deep down I was a good human being.

He was wrong.

Right now, all I feel is dirty and evil. As I cry for a man from my past while I sit here naked for a man who has no part of my future, my skin begins to crawl. I want to get out of it. I want to wash every mistake—the past and the current—from my body.

I fly off my bed and into my bathroom as fast as I can, not even bothering to put something on me for the walk from my room to the basement bathroom.

My mind doesn't stop to consider if there's somebody down here or not. All it can register is the fact that I am so dirty and gross and damaged that I have to wash it, scratch it, remove it from my body.

The bathroom door slams behind me as another sob breaks from my body. I can't get to the shower quick enough. My hand shakes as I push the nozzle as hot as it will go. Water sputters out of the shower head. I don't wait for the water to warm before I climb in and let it run down my body.

The tears won't stop coming. No matter how many times I tell myself I don't deserve to grieve—or feel anything—it still comes.

The sound of a door shutting pulls me from my memories. And now I have to wonder if someone was down here. If someone in my present just witnessed this breaking. This thing I try to hide so fiercely.

The hot water stings my skin. I relish it as the night before gets washed from my body.

I can almost feel Connor's memories getting washed from my mind.

Almost.

15

MAVERICK

MY FEET HURRY up the basement stairs, racing like I can't get out of here fast enough. The coffee mug in my hand splatters hot coffee everywhere, dripping down my hand and onto the carpet. I fiddle with the doorknob, slamming the basement door behind me. I hastily slam the coffee cup on the kitchen counter and then beeline for my room. I have enough mind not to slam the bedroom door, and I push it shut softly before resting my forehead against it as I gather my thoughts.

Aspen and Selma are both gone—*thank fuck*.

I had gone downstairs to see if Veronica was home or not. My eyes were scanning over a newspaper at the kitchen bar this morning when Tristan made the walk of shame. He opened the door to the basement with a shit eating grin on his face. There was no shame, only pure glee. His hair was all over the place, making it evident that Veronica's hands had run through it and pulled it every which way. His clothes were wrinkled, probably from being on the ground all night.

When they were whispering to each other last night, I wasn't expecting them to leave the game halfway through it.

I went with a warm cup of coffee in hand to see if she was downstairs this morning.

My foot was about to step off the last stair when I heard the first sob. It stopped me in my place, my foot midair. I thought my ears were playing tricks on me. I didn't think Veronica was capable of having an emotion as strong as the despair echoing through the basement. Another sob came. My hand clenched the coffee mug, my stomach doing the same. The heart wrenching sound pulled at something inside me.

Veronica's bedroom door swung open next and I took a step back at the image I saw.

She was completely naked, not a strip of clothing on her. I barely noticed her body. My eyes were too busy taking in the turmoil on her face. Grief was written in every line. The wetness of her cheeks and neck glistened under the basement lights as she ran to the bathroom. The door slammed and a few seconds later, I heard the sound of the shower turning on.

Even though the basement was no longer silent, filled with the sound of cascading water, I could still hear the sounds of her crying over the noise. My mind told me to move, to run up the stairs and pretend nothing happened, but my body wouldn't move from that last step.

I was trying to process it all. The tears that ran down her face, covering her neck. The way she was scratching at her body. The way her body shook with grief. I couldn't unsee it. I couldn't wipe it from my brain.

The next sob set me on edge, shook me from my thoughts. I ran up the stairs like a bat out of hell, barely registering that my hand was getting burnt by the hot coffee sloshing around. Now, my forehead is resting against the cold wooden door. My heart slams against my chest, my mind racing in every direction.

My hands are on either side of my head, pushing against the door like I'm trying to push the thoughts away. But I can't shake it.

I wonder if Tristan did this to her. If I find out he had something to do with this kind of sorrow, I will probably lose my shit. I've never felt this kind of anger toward anybody before besides Selma's father.

Whoever broke her down like this has my fists clenching against the door—and I don't even know why.

I can still hear the sound of the running water beneath me. I wonder if she's still in there, falling apart. I try not to acknowledge the fact that the sight of endless tears running down her cheeks has unraveled me like this.

Selma's tears make me feel protective.

Veronica's tears have just gutted me.

Maybe it's because I had her pinned so well in my mind. The ice queen. The brat. The girl who wants nothing to do with anyone. Maybe it's because I'm just now realizing how wrong I was. There is something in there, deep inside of her, that *hurts*. So loudly, it rumbles the whole house.

I'm still internally losing my shit when the water turns off. I imagine her wiping her tears and drying off with a towel. If I was a betting guy, I'd surmise that Veronica will get dressed and zip that sadness up like she zips up her pink combat boots. That she will come upstairs and keep pretending she has no feelings whatsoever.

Not wanting to miss her when she decides to come up—in case she wants to talk about it—I grab my laptop and set up shop on our living room couch. I'm anxious, my fingers drumming against my knee, my heart thundering in my chest.

Twenty minutes go by before I hear her soft footsteps coming up the stairs.

I start typing on my laptop, pretending to be busy. The words that fill the screen don't even make sense, but she won't know that.

"Good morning," I mumble, keeping my eyes on my computer screen and not on her.

She doesn't respond, choosing to walk into the kitchen and rifle around instead. I sneak a glance once I feel like she's busy enough to not notice me looking at her. Her back is to me as she reaches into the cabinet for a bowl. Her long hair is wet and tangled down her back.

When she makes her next motion, I train my eyes back on the laptop in front of me. The sound of cereal being dumped into the ceramic bowl fills my ears. That and the sound of my fingers racing against the keyboard, still forming jumbled words.

"What happened to your hand?" she asks.

My eyes shoot up and find her standing right next to me—so close I can smell her shampoo or body wash. I look down at my hand, following her gaze, and find bright red splotches on my skin.

Burns from the coffee.

The coffee I spilled after you spilled your heart out.

Part of me wants to lie and make up a story about where I got it from. But I can't. Because seeing her in pain like that makes me feel like I have to ask her if she's okay. "I spilled coffee on it. Look, I had gone downstairs to check on you and I—"

"I won't talk about it, Maverick." Her spoon circles around in her bowl before she picks it up and shovels a bite into her mouth.

"Veronica—"

"I said no. You weren't supposed to be down there, anyway," she states.

I set the laptop down on the ottoman and stand up. We are almost toe-to-toe, her cereal bowl the only barrier between the two of us. My eyes look over her, taking in her blank expression, trying to see if she's okay. Veronica's hair is sopping wet, like she didn't even have it in her to dry it. The whites of her eyes are bloodshot and even her strained voice gives her away. It's hoarse, scratching at the end of her sentences.

My hands run through my hair, trying to keep themselves busy. There are a million responses that go through my mind, but only one comes out. "But I was, Veronica. And I can't pretend I didn't just witness that. So—"

"So, what?" she bites out, slamming her bowl of cereal down on the end table. Her arms cross over her chest.

"You were fucking sad!" I shout, losing my cool. I pull a long breath in through my nose, trying to gain some composure. The air escapes back out of my lips, slowly. I feel bad for yelling, but her icy demeanor is driving me insane. For once, I want her to just stop this charade she has going that everything is fine, and admit to someone that she isn't okay. Even if it's me. Someone she hardly knows.

A sad laugh escapes her lips before she shakes her head and retreats across the room. Before she makes it to the door that leads back downstairs, I dodge the ottoman and follow her.

In front of the door, she spins around. "So now I'm sad?

That's great, Maverick. Just call me pathetic next time, won't you?"

"Don't try and twist my words. You and I both know what I meant by that. You didn't look pathetic. You looked sad. And you know what, Veronica? It's okay to be fucking sad. It's okay to have demons. It's okay to admit to one fucking person that you have feelings that aren't just vain or selfish or shallow." I walk closer to her now, retreating into her personal space, but just barely.

Her small chest rises and falls. I'm ready for her to lash out at me. That seems to be her MO. I brace myself for it, but her only response is the sag of her body.

"You don't want to know my demons." Her blue eyes find mine and there's no longer anger in them. It isn't even sadness, but defeat. Her eyelashes are wet and clumped together. Unshed tears making her blue eyes glassy.

Instinctively, I reach out to touch her. I place my hands on her shoulders. I want to shake the truth from her. "What if I do?" I take a step back from her after realizing how close we are.

"If you did, you wouldn't want to be friends with me, let alone have me as a roommate," Veronica mumbles quietly, looking down at her bare feet.

"You underestimate me. From where I stand, it seems like you *need* a friend." I don't even realize my fingers are tapping against my thigh until her eyes focus on them.

"We can be friends, Maverick, but I'm not telling you anything. Today, or maybe ever." She takes a long breath. "I've had enough of my past. I can't dwell on it any longer."

"Just tell me if Tristan hurt you." I pin her with my gaze, as though daring her to look away from me.

She lets out a small laugh. "I'm not the victim in anybody's story. I'm the villain."

With that, she opens the door to the basement and retreats to her room.

I'm left staring at her soggy cereal, wondering what her last comment could possibly mean.

16

VERONICA

I FALL into a steady rhythm for the next few weeks. My time is filled between school, work, and hanging out with my roommates. Lily somehow convinced me to go to the last two Thirsty Thursdays at Lenny's—and they weren't so bad. I even celebrated Halloween with all of them.

It wasn't my ideal scenario, but at least I tried.

Maverick and I have fallen into an odd almost-friendship. He tries to get me to divulge more and more about myself every day—a side effect, I think, from watching me crumble. At first, I was uncomfortable with it. I didn't want his pity, or anyone else's. But for some reason, I shared a little. And I realized how fucking *good* it felt to not keep every single little thing to myself.

I still haven't told him about what led to the breakdown. What haunts me at night. What makes me wake up in cold sweats after a nightmare of reliving the worst night of my life. We aren't that close, and I don't ever plan for us to be.

It's a Tuesday night, and a large part of me doesn't want to go downstairs and fall asleep to whatever hell my mind will bring me to tonight. So, I'm sitting on the couch watching old game shows.

Selma went to bed two hours ago, claiming she had a long day at work and has the early shift again tomorrow. Aspen watched an episode with me earlier before going out for the night. And I have no idea where Maverick is.

I'm in the midst of dozing off when the front door opens and Maverick walks in. It causes me to jump, sending the remote flying. The picture from the TV is the only source of light in the living room. He sets his keys in the bowl beside the door and walks to the kitchen, mumbling a *hi* to me on his way. I hear him poke around in the refrigerator before he heads toward me, two beer bottles clutched in his hands.

He sits on the other side of the couch, a comfortable distance away from me. I look over to watch him take a long pull of his beer. As soon as he looks over at me, I quickly focus back on the TV, an old episode of Family Feud playing. I wipe at my mouth, making sure there's no drool from my brief nap.

I wish there was more sound coming from the TV to fill the silence of the room, but the remote fell behind the couch when Maverick walked in and I'm too lazy to get up and look for it.

Maverick pops the top off one of the beer bottles and holds it out to me. "You know Aspen thinks you hate him. Either that or you're playing hard to get."

His voice causes me to jump, a bit of beer flying from the top of my bottle and onto my collarbone.

I don't look away from the TV, where Steve Harvey raises his eyebrows and shakes his head at a contestant's answer. "I'm certainly not playing hard to get."

I watch from the corner of my eye as he stretches out his long legs. "Then you do hate him?" He's staring at me, jostling his beer bottle with his hand.

"No. Why would I hate him?" I take a long swig from my own beer, avoiding looking at Maverick.

"Because you don't talk to him like you talk to me." He shifts again, which finally draws my eyes in his direction.

When I turn my head, I find his body angled toward mine and his blue eyes glowing in the light of the TV, staring straight at me.

"Oh, that's easy. It's because you're taken." I shrug, taking another swig from the bottle. The beer tastes like piss, but I won't complain right now. It's something to keep me busy. And I'm searching for the numb.

His dark eyebrows raise as he thinks my words through. I give him the amount of time he needs, not wanting to elaborate if I don't have to.

He nods slowly and says, "Well, yeah, but what's that have to do with Aspen?"

"He's single." I take another sip from my beer, letting the bitter taste of the Heineken linger on my tongue before swallowing.

"Just because he's single doesn't mean you can't be nice to the guy," Maverick says.

"Wait a minute. Just because I'm not eating out of the palm of his hand doesn't mean I'm not nice to him. I just don't want to give him the idea that I might be interested in him."

"I still don't understand."

I drag my eyes away from the Viagra commercial to look back at Maverick. "You're in a very happy relationship. There is no chance of you falling in love with me or getting attached or wanting more in any capacity. So, *we* can be friends."

"You won't be friends with a single guy because there's a chance they might get feelings for you?" he asks.

"Yep," I deadpan, popping the *p*.

"Aren't you thinking a little highly of yourself?" he counters.

I shrug, finishing off the last of my beer. It clinks against the table when I set it down on the end table next to me. "Maybe, but if I think there's a chance a guy is attracted to me then I won't be friends with him. There's a small chance after attraction that the person can fall in love and I don't want anyone falling in love with me."

"So, we're officially friends?" he asks with a smirk.

I reach over and pull on his hoodie string, pulling it tight and then letting it go. It recoils from my hand and bounces against his face. "Hell, we could be *best* friends. You're so disgustingly in love with Selma that you'd never find me attractive. It's a win-win situation."

He slowly swallows. For the first time, I'm close enough to him to spot it. Starting under his bottom lip and roaming over to the skin above his top lip, there's a jagged line. A scar. An imperfection. I itch to paint it, unable to look away. I'm too busy memorizing the way it slopes down. My brain ponders how I've never seen it before. Maybe I just never looked at him hard enough.

I'm still staring at that scar when he hesitantly smiles and jokes, "Best friends, then?"

My eyes pull away from his lips and find his eyes. The smile that overtakes my face is completely genuine. I hold out my hand and wait for his to engulf my own. His is warm; mine is cold.

"BFFs," I joke back, shaking our hands up and down once before pulling my hand back. We stay in a stare-down for a few moments before I pop off the couch, leaving my empty bottle on the table, and make my way to the door to the basement.

As I open the door, I look over my shoulder to find Maverick staring after me, an unreadable look covering his face.

I hope he knows I was joking.

17

MAVERICK

"Oh my god, this can't be real." Veronica leans over my shoulder as we scroll through our professor's Facebook page. She's so close I can smell the sweet flowery scent of her perfume.

A contradiction I have come to know about her.

She smells so sweet, a contradiction of her sour attitude.

"Maverick, are you seeing this?" Her hair hits me in the face as she leans even more over me, her finger touching my laptop screen.

Our professor is in head to toe My Little Pony gear. It's basically cosplay of a rainbow pony. His face is even smothered in sparkly shit. His wife and kids are posing in the picture with him, all of them dressed as different ponies.

"I mean, holy fuck. This is amazing!" Veronica goes back to her chair a few feet away from me, chuckling to herself.

"Shh!" a feisty student directs at her from across the library.

Veronica makes a face back at the shusher.

I laugh under my breath, shaking my head. Judging by the way Veronica glares at the girl, she's thinking of a way to rile her up even more.

"Ready to get back to studying?" I ask her, trying to pull her eyes away from the girl and back on me. It's a nice afternoon and while the weather is almost perfect outside, Veronica and I

are both holed up in the library studying for our upcoming sociology midterm.

"What are you thinking about?" Veronica asks, causing me
to jump.

I bite down hard on the pen I didn't realize I was chewing
on. The pen makes a cracking noise. I look down at it, making
sure I didn't just make it explode. When I'm sure it isn't bleeding
ink everywhere, I throw it down onto our large table.

Looking across the table, I find the start of a doodle on her
notepad. Before she realizes what I'm doing, I grab it from the
table and take it to examine further.

"Maverick! Give that back right now." Veronica shoots out
of her chair and tries to grab it from my hand, but I have an
iron grip.

My eyes glide over what she was drawing. It's a pair of eyes
filled with unshed tears. I'm amazed at the amount of detail,
done with just her pencil. The eyes seem kind, genuine, like
they're staring into my soul. The more I look, the more details I
notice. In the pupils, there are small waves.

"This is incredible, Veronica," I tell her, pulling it away from
her reach when she lunges for it again. I go to flip through the
rest of the notepad and notice many drawings of different
features. There are hands, a nose, eyebrows, freckles, moles. As
the pages flutter, I see the same pair of eyes—over and over
again. They're always sad.

Finally, when I'm too busy staring at her art—the beautiful
lines and curves of the drawings—she rips the notepad from my
hand. I'm about to compliment her further when she storms
away from me. The only thing she has in her hand is the
notepad, the rest of her belongings still strewn about all over the
table I'm now alone at.

I jump out of my chair, making eye contact with some of the
people glaring at us. I ignore them and rush in the direction she
went. She's weaving in and out of bookshelves, going deeper
into our campus library.

I finally catch her in a dim corner. "Veronica," I say quietly,
grabbing her by the elbow. I go to turn her toward me and
what's on her face absolutely destroys me.

It's hurt. It's raw. It's real. But most of all, it's betrayal—betrayal I put there.

My heart drops to my feet. I've never been looked at in the way she's looking at me right now. And in this moment, I know whatever I just came across in that notepad is more than just pretty doodles to her. The drawings are another jagged piece of her puzzle I can't seem to put together.

I know the right thing to do right now is comfort her. To drop it. To apologize and ask her how I can fix the mistake I just made. That's what I would do for any of my friends. That's what I've always done for them. But I can't. I have to know more. So instead of pulling her in, comforting her and dropping it, I slide the blade in further.

"What are those, Veronica?" My hand is still gently wrapped around her slender arm.

She uses the arm I'm not holding to clench the notepad closer to her chest. You would think by the way it's pressed against her that she thinks I'm about to rip it from her hands and destroy it.

A tear falls from her eye. One single tear. I track its movement down the slope of her cheek, off her chin and onto the black sweatshirt she's wearing. It drips right next to a paint stain.

"They're imperfections," she whispers, not looking away from me.

"Imperfections?" My mind reels with what she means. I look away from her crystal-blue eyes, glossy with unshed tears, and look at the book cradled against her chest.

"I draw—well, I prefer to paint—imperfections." Her voice is stronger now, as though she's gaining her composure back.

I know the moment of me getting information from her is fleeting.

"Why?" I ask, my voice gravelly and low, trying not to interrupt the fragile bubble we're currently in.

She leans back against the bookshelf. "Because it's what I do. I find imperfections. I paint them. I put them out into the world forever." Her eyes glance to my lips for a split second.

For some reason, it sends a shock through me—something a guy in a relationship shouldn't be feeling.

There could be a thousand people staring at us in this library right now, and I wouldn't care.

I will rip this truth from her no matter what it takes, no matter who is watching.

"Whose eyes are they?" I know the moment it leaves my mouth that I have finally asked the right question—or the wrong one. Because we're both staring into each other's eyes, I can see the moment my words register within her.

They flash with despair.

With guilt?

She tries to step back, but she can't. We're in a corner, with nobody around and no space for her to retreat. She has the bookshelf against her back and me in front of her, and I will not waver.

It's silent for a long time, both of us still staring at the other, testing to see who will be the one to break first.

"Connor's." It comes out a whisper, it's so quiet.

If we weren't in a library or if I wasn't so close to her, I wouldn't have even heard it. "Who is Connor?"

"Connor is my boyfriend."

"You have a boyfriend?" I ask, bewildered by this information.

"I did. He died."

A breath escapes my body, loudly and uncontrollably. I feel like the biggest dick in the world. I've made her tell me this secret of hers, expecting it to be something entirely different. I didn't expect her to have lost somebody so close to her. She's told me from the day we met that she wasn't looking for something serious—ever. I thought it was because some douchebag broke her heart, but the little amount I thought I knew about Veronica was all wrong.

"I'm sorry." I don't know what else to say. I've never had somebody close to me die. I haven't ever had to face death, and I'm not sure what the appropriate way to respond is when someone tells me they've lost someone.

She steps closer to me. Those damn boots are on her feet again, making her already tall frame even taller. We aren't completely eye-to-eye, but she's definitely close enough to look me dead in the eye.

"Don't be sorry, Maverick. I was the reason he died." She stands there for a long moment.

I can't estimate how long because my mind is too busy processing what she just said.

Just when I finally have my thoughts together enough to ask her what she meant, she steps away from me and disappears into the shelves again.

This time, I don't chase her.

18

VERONICA

THREE YEARS AGO

"Do you love me?" I sit in the passenger seat of my car, tears streaming down my face. I don't dare look over at him. I can't let him see the tears rolling down my cheeks. I look out the window, at all the happy beachgoers. Even though the sun is setting, there's still a fair amount of people spread out along the shore.

"Of course I love you. Why are you even asking?" He reaches over to rest his hand on my knee, and squeezes—a silent plea for me to look at him.

But I don't. "I saw the way you were looking at her." I try to hide the hurt in my voice.

"Looking at *who*?"

I don't answer, in disbelief that he doesn't even know who I'm talking about.

"Damn it, Veronica, look at me." His hand lifts from my knee and gently forces my chin to face him.

Luckily, the tears no longer fall. All that's left is anger. "You know who!"

He jumps when I yell—the only thing that gives away his feelings. His face stays stone cold. Connor's voice is a calm whisper when he says, "I have no idea what you're talking about."

"Louisa! Louisa Finn. I saw the way you were looking at her tonight. Is that what you're into? A five foot, dark-haired, *her*?!"

His eyes widen, his fingers lightly strumming the steering wheel, which I know he does when he's anxious. "I have no idea what narrative you've written in your head, but I have zero interest in her. I'm in love with you!"

I laugh—a shrill noise that fills the silence of the car. "Okay, Connor. Next joke, please." I hastily unbuckle my seatbelt and force the car door open. Slamming it, I speed toward a secluded part of the beach. I know he's following me when another door slams.

"Veronica! Don't just walk away from me," he yells, his own anger now filling in the spaces between each syllable.

Sand gets in my Converse shoes, irritating the hell out of me. I stop to yank both of them off, throwing them onto the sand.

I keep walking until the water hits my feet. The wave rolls in, engulfing my feet for a few short moments before it retreats back.

Connor's hand wraps around my elbow, spinning me to look at him. "What have I ever done to make you think I want anyone other than you? I love you *so* much. I don't look at other girls. All I want is you."

His eyes are sad and pleading, the greens of his irises popping against the freckles that dust his nose and cheeks. I want to kiss him so badly, to forget about this stupid fight, but I don't because I know what I saw when I saw him looking at her.

"And Louisa Finn," I retort.

He lets out an exasperated sigh, rolling his eyes as he does so. I can tell he's annoyed when he runs a hand over his face, pulling the skin. "What do you want from me right now?"

His chest heaves up and down, his gaze penetrating my own. I won't back down and neither will he.

When I take a long breath in, I smell the sweet salty scent of the ocean. Every few seconds, the sound of the waves crashing against the shore fills my ears. "I want you to not look at other girls!"

He laughs. "Holy hell, Veronica. I don't! You've come up

with this bat-shit crazy idea in your head that I'm looking at other girls, so you can have a reason to be mad at me. You want me to grovel at your feet, to apologize and tell you every reason I love you, so you feel better about yourself. Why are you so insecure? Don't you see how perfect you are?"

When I don't respond, he turns around and starts to walk right into the ocean—away from me. He's running away from me. I feel my lip start to tremble, an easy indicator that I won't be able to hold back the tears much longer.

"I do not!" I snap, but it comes out as more of a whine. I think about arguing with him, trying to convince him he's wrong. But I know deep down he's right. I *am* insecure and I need to find ways to fight with him to have him say sweet things to me and make me feel good about myself.

"Yes, you are! If you would just step out of your head for two seconds and think about someone other than yourself for once, you would see that I'm head over heels in love with you. I love every bitchy, insecure, selfish part of you. Because I know the *real* you. The one who's sweet and funny and passionate. I love both sides to you, but I'm not going to let you attack me for something I didn't do." He's even farther from me now, his clothes starting to stick to his skin from the water.

"Fine! If I'm so insecure and such a bitch, then let's end it," I yell.

I can't see the look on his face, but I do notice the way he freezes. The way his lean muscles tighten underneath his shirt. His shoulders rise in a deep breath before he turns around and a sarcastic laugh passes through his lips as his eyes widen maniacally. "Holy shit. *That's* what you're latching onto from everything I just said? I'm done, Veronica. Done!" he yells.

My stomach turns at his last word. He's my life. I can't lose him. But I'm too stubborn to actually say that.

"Then go!" I walk deeper into the water. The warm water laps against my knees. "This was never supposed to be serious anyway, right? You just wanted to find out what's behind *East Point's princess*. What really makes her tick. If she's really such a bitch or if she's just damaged. If it's all a persona she puts on to keep people away. Well congrats, Connor Liams, you found out.

You cracked open my shell and discovered what's really underneath." I have to yell even louder than before so he can hear me with how far away he is. I start to slow clap as I engulf myself even deeper into the water. Now, I'm all the way in, the water lapping against my belly button.

"Get out of the water, Veronica," he says, taking a few steps closer to me so he doesn't have to yell as much. Even after a few steps toward me, we're still a good distance apart.

"You first, Connor. Why should I get out if you're still in?" I know it's childish, but I turn my back to him and walk in even deeper. "You know, you did good. Not only did you get to see what was beneath the surface, you got me to fall in love with you. Veronica Cunningham, the heartless bitch, actually *can* fall in love. Make sure to post it to Facebook! And don't forget about Instagram, Twitter, and Snapchat."

"Turn around," Connor begs.

I turn around and find him closer than he was before. I don't hide the tears that roam freely down my cheeks. "All I wanted was a fairytale. But the villains don't ever get that, do they?" My voice cracks. I'm not sure if it's possible, but I hate myself even more in this moment. I'm not even a good villain at this point, I'm just a whiny and insecure girl.

"Just talk to me." His voice is hoarse, defeated—and I feel his pain straight to my bones. "I love you. I don't care that you aren't perfect, I just don't want you accusing me all the damn time." Even though the sun is setting, I can see his green eyes under the blond lashes that frame them. I can see the anguish on his face.

It makes my heart hurt, but it makes my needful brain happy. I want to drive him crazy. I want to make him hurt. I want him to prove his love to me.

I can almost feel my heart reaching out for him from inside my chest. I almost get out, hoping he'll follow me, but I'm stubborn and he's embarrassed me. Maybe I had overreacted, letting my insecurities get in the way of our relationship, but I won't admit that.

So, I take one last look at him, capturing the way he looks right now, feeling the itch to paint him.

The despair on his face is beautiful.

Am I fucked up for thinking it's beautiful?

Call me a bitch, but I think it is.

I take the mental snapshot and fall back into the water. I hear him yell right before my face goes under water, but I take my time coming back up.

When I finally do break the surface of the water, Connor is racing toward me—the water now up to his hips—and gaining on me fast.

"Get away from me! We're ending this right now. You can leave now." I slowly begin to walk backward, my toes squishing in the sand beneath my feet. I'm good at faking things, so the forced boredom in my tone hits home judging by the look on his face.

He runs a hand through the long, curly waves of the mop that is his hair. "God, you're so crazy sometimes."

His words send a spear right through my heart, and in that moment, I swear I can feel my chest being stabbed over and over. Rage quickly replaces the hurt—my favorite defense mechanism.

There she is.

I almost smile. I'd rather be pissed off than hurt any day. "Then leave, Connor! Turn around and get in your car and never speak to me again because I'm *so* damn crazy." Tears escape my eyes even against my sheer willpower to keep them in. "I am crazy! Loving you makes me absolutely crazy and you're right. I can't explain it, but I *am* crazy."

He steps closer to me, his hand outspread and reaching for me.

I almost let him touch me. I almost give up the fight and run into his arms—the only place I ever want to be anymore.

"Veronica…" His voice is just a whisper above the waves.

All I hear is pity. Not love, not hurt, just pity. And that's the worst thing of all.

So just before his outspread fingers find my skin and make me forget why we were even fighting to begin with, I dive my head under the water, letting the cold wash over me.

When I resurface, he's in the same spot, glaring at me.

There's so much *anger* on his face. I hate that I put it there, but I don't hate it as much as he's made me feel.

"Fine, Veronica. Two can play that game." He swims into the water, but instead of diving toward the shore, he goes deeper into the ocean. Away from me, and even farther then I am from the shore.

I dive in to find him, but I can't see anything. The sun has now set, making it almost impossible to see a thing. I want to find him, to tell him he can't go that far into the ocean when the tide is like this. He knows better. We've been told about the dangers of the ocean since we were learning the alphabet. Kids that live by the water are always told these things.

My eyes burn from the salt water as I try to find him. My chest starts to feel heavy, alerting me to the fact that I need air. I stay down a few seconds longer and look around before I finally push against the squishy ocean floor and send myself up. My head breaks through the water. I push my long hair out of my face, looking around in the dark for him.

"Connor?" I ask quietly, while treading water. I keep moving forward until my feet hit the ground. I keep walking until half my body is out of the water. "Connor!" I say louder this time, scanning the expanse of the beach and the water as I search for him.

My heart starts pounding in my chest. I don't see him anywhere. I calculate in my head if he had enough time to get out of the water and make it all the way back to his car in the minute I was under water.

It's possible, but in my gut, I know he wouldn't leave me like that.

Where is he?

There is a loud splash and I quickly spin to see him break through the waves. My heart plummets.

"Ronnie!" he yells, struggling against the water. His arms wave in the air, slapping against the water in a torturous sound.

I'm making my way toward him as fast as I can when he goes underneath again. I scream, quickly pumping my arms and legs in the water to try and make it to him.

But he doesn't come up.

It's taking too long for him to come up.

Where the hell is he?!

I frantically dive below the surface of the water repeatedly, feeling the water around me for any part of his body. Each time, I come up with nothing.

My eyes are stinging from opening them so many times in the water. My lungs are burning from screaming and from holding my breath for so long.

Something bumps against my foot. When I go under the water, I find that it's a body. I tug on it with all the power I can muster while still treading water. I don't know how I do it, but somehow, I pull and swim hard enough to get him onto the shore of the beach.

It's there that I find a mass of people standing.

"Call nine-one-one!" I plead, dragging Connor up the shore enough to get him out of the strongest part of the tide.

A man comes to the other side of Connor and helps me pull him. We both look down.

He isn't breathing.

No part of him is moving.

His clothes are wet on his skin, clasping to every inch of him like they themselves are trying to suffocate him.

"Oh my god," I say, when it fully registers to me that his chest isn't moving. My knees drop to the sand. Before I even realize what I'm doing, I'm pushing against his chest. I count the beats in my head. Once I've reached the amount of chest compressions I've been taught to do, I tilt his head back and breathe air into him.

When nothing happens, I start back over.

Over and over.

Over and over.

Push, push, breathe, breathe.

Nothing, nothing...

There are people around me, where a large crowd has now gathered. They all watch as I desperately push against Connor's chest. I'm trying so hard to bring life back into him. To get him to breathe.

I just need one breath. He has to wake up. He has to come back.

Push, push, breathe, breathe.

Nothing, nothing.

Tears stream down my face now, a torrential downpour of tears mixing with the salty droplets of ocean that are all over his body. My arms are shaking, starting to give out from my endless attempts to save him. "Damn it, Connor!" I scream, pushing so hard against his sternum I'm convinced I've broken something by now.

And still, nothing happens.

The love of my life is lifeless in front of me.

A strong hand lands on my shoulder and I look up to see the face of a paramedic. Someone else from his team pulls me off Connor and resumes the compressions I was just frantically giving. I scramble in the sand, trying to find my way back to Connor.

I have to help them.

I have to bring him back to life.

He can't leave me.

The team does the same thing I was doing.

Push, push, breathe, breathe.

Nothing, nothing.

Every part of me dies when they pronounce him dead. My soul is ripped right out of me and thrown into the ocean.

Connor is dead.

Because of me.

19

VERONICA

I DO what I always do. I flee. At first, I walk around aimlessly for what seems like *hours*. While I walk around the campus, my head runs rampant with my past. Every memory Connor and I made the year we were together flashes through my mind.

The way he made me feel.

The way I felt when he died.

The way I haven't felt since.

The way I feel again, because of Maverick.

Because of stupid, considerate, compassionate, Maverick.

I wasn't supposed to feel like this again. I wasn't supposed to feel anything. I shouldn't be feeling anything. The moment that Connor lost his life in front of me—*because* of me—I lost any chance at feeling this way again. I don't deserve it. I don't want it.

All I do is destroy. I'm a toxic person. My love is poison. I've poisoned one person already, enough for him to lose his life over it. I won't let it happen again.

The months that turned into years after Connor's death were all awful.

Connor's parents were devastated. Everyone looked at me differently. They either pitied me or blamed me for Connor's death. My parents continuously tried to tell me it wasn't my fault, but they weren't there. They didn't realize he wouldn't have been in the water if it weren't for my childish games.

I didn't hold him under the water until his lungs gave out, but I might as well have.

I survived—barely—in that town for three years before I had to leave. After taking online college courses for an extended amount of time, I told my parents I was going to college thousands of miles away. Then I left, saying goodbye to no one other than them.

My feet now take me to Lenny's of their own accord. I'd been too lost in my thoughts to even figure out where I was drifting to. I look around the dive bar, trying to clear my head.

When Maverick had asked me what happened to Connor, I panicked. I didn't want to tell him what I'd done. I didn't want him to look at me the same way the people in my whole hometown did. Like I was this disease. I didn't want to see the disappointment in his eyes—the disgust. But at the same time, I almost *want* to divulge this secret to him.

I want to rip my heart open, let him look at every broken and dark piece of me. I want him to take a magnifying glass to every cut and bruise against my heart. The consequences of my actions written all over my soul. I want to know if he'd still want to be my friend once he's seen it all.

He shouldn't want to stay close to me after knowing.

I won't let him stay close to me after knowing.

Lenny's is considerably empty. There are the regulars lining the bar, some of them having hushed conversations with one another, but most are just staring into their half-empty drinks. For a brief moment, I wonder what each of their stories are.

Are they drunks?

Have they gone through a monumental loss like I have?

I realize I don't really care. My grief still overwhelms me so much it's hard for me to even fathom someone else's life being as bad as mine.

My selfishness killed Connor. And yet, I can't stop being selfish. I can't imagine someone else feels the kind of pain I do when I look back at that night. Maybe it's the fact that my pain is magnified by my guilt over it all.

Lenny nods at me from behind the counter as I walk past him to the back booth. I slide across the worn, red vinyl seat. A slow depressing song plays over the speakers as I look around. This very booth is where we sat when Lily convinced me to go out with the group for the first time. I sat in this same spot and watched Maverick and Selma have an intimate conversation, blind to the people around them.

In that instant, I hated them.

They had each other. They were alive.

I'd sat there glaring at them until Lily lightly elbowed me. The look she'd given me had been unreadable. In the moment, I had wondered if she thought I was jealous.

I was, but not for the reasons she probably thought.

Now, I scrape at the worn wood of the table. Every inch of it is covered in writing. I'm lost in my thoughts until I sense someone walk up to the table.

"Nothing for me tonight, Len," I say, not bothering to look up. Len couldn't give a shit if I looked him in the eye or not, so I don't. It's unnecessary.

"Well, that's great," a voice responds, but it's not Lenny's.

I lazily drag my eyes away from the table to the man standing a few feet away from me. I sigh and say, "What are you doing here, Maverick?"

His hands are tucked into the pockets of his dark jeans. He ignores me, pulling down the hood of his sweatshirt and sliding in right next to me. His dark hair sticks up in various directions.

"You know there's a whole open side over there, right?" I ask, looking to the other side of the booth while sliding to the very end of it—as close to the wall as I can get to get away from him.

He just grunts, obviously ignoring my comment. He angles his body so he's facing me. "Why'd you come here of all places?" His blue eyes seem dull under the fluorescent lighting.

I don't answer him at first. I don't owe him any sort of explanation as to why I'm here. If I'm being honest, I don't even know why I'm here. After what happened in the library earlier, I just had to walk. And walking led me here.

"Veronica?" he pushes.

I bring my gaze to his, rolling my eyes. "I came here because I wanted to."

Maverick nods. He runs a finger over his bottom lip in concentration. "But why did you want to?"

It's now that I notice he's holding my bag I left behind at the library. I snatch it from his hands quickly, shoving it into the corner of the booth.

I huff, maddened that he keeps asking questions. "I'm an adult who can do whatever the hell I want to, Maverick. I'm here because I want to be here. You don't need to read into it."

The sound of glasses clinking mixes with the melancholy playlist of the bar. Maverick opens his mouth to say something but instead, closes it. If I cared about him, or about *anything*, I'd wonder what he was about to ask. But I don't. So instead, I look around the bar.

"What happened at the library?" His voice is quiet and hesitant. I wonder if he sat on the same side of the booth as me so I wouldn't be able to escape him like I did in the library.

"I don't want to talk about it, Maverick." I look at him for a brief moment, my eyes pleading for him to drop it. We hold the moment for a little bit longer before I pull my eyes away from him.

Dollar bills cover every surface of the walls. Some have faces drawn on them where others have sayings or names printed on them. There are a few blank ones. I wonder why someone would go to the trouble of sticking their dollar to the wall without even signing it.

Did they feel insignificant? Like their name wasn't even worth remembering?

Like me?

When I look away from the walls, I find Maverick staring at me. "Why are you here?" I ask for the second time tonight. This time I stare at him until he gives me an answer.

He runs a hand through his hair. "Selma sent me."

I raise my eyebrows at him, instantly recognizing the lie. Selma is a nice girl—overly nice even—but she doesn't care that much about my whereabouts. Plus, unless he told her about our little episode at the library, she would have zero reason to be worried about me.

"Mmm, and why is that?" I ask, turning my body to face his, but still pressing my back against the wall to keep a distance.

He fidgets, alerting me to the fact that he's noticeably uncomfortable, those long fingers tapping against his thigh doing nothing to dissuade my assumption.

It rips at my heart.

Connor used to do that.

"The way we left things in the library...I hated it. I sat at home waiting for you to get there, anxious and worried. I just needed to know if you were okay," Maverick says.

"I'm never okay, Maverick." I lean in closer and make sure to look him right in the eye when I say this.

I can tell it confuses him by the way his dark eyebrows furrow together. He looks down, and before I can retreat back into my safe space against the wall, his finger is almost pressed against my skin.

"What does this say?" he asks.

My body betrays me and lets out a shiver with his almost-touch. His narrow finger gestures to the words inked over my heart. I want to get as far away from him as possible, but I can't move, and worse, my heartbeat quickens to a speed that I know he must feel.

When I don't answer, he slowly brushes my long hair off my shoulder, allowing him a full view of the tattoo, his fingertip still hovering over the start of it. Finally, I get in the right mind to back away, but only by an inch.

We are still close—too close. I wish to be anywhere but in this dingy booth with him. Not even the sound of the broken speakers or the clanking of beer bottles can lower the loud rush of blood pumping through my veins.

My heart shouldn't quicken for anyone anymore. It died right along with Connor. But here it is, doing just that for a boy who drives me insane most of the time.

A boy with a very serious long-term girlfriend.

"Destroy what destroys you," he murmurs, but I barely hear him over the sound of the sad music.

His eyes find mine and they look sad. And for the first time in a long time, I feel bad for being the reason for someone's sadness.

"What does that even mean, Veronica?" he asks.

My throat closes up with more memories of Connor.

The feeling of my hand wrapped in his.

His lips, his love.

His death.

I don't want to be here, but Maverick sits on the outside of the booth and it would take effort to get out—effort I simply don't have right now. I know my only way out and away from Maverick is to give him what he wants.

"It means what it says, no more and no less. Destroy what destroys you."

"And what has destroyed you?" he asks, his words strained.

It's a small gesture, a platonic one even, but when his soothing hand rests against my shoulder, I start to panic.

Not because he's touching me—but because I like it.

"Love, Maverick. Love destroyed me."

He winces as soon as the nasty four-letter word leaves my mouth, as if what I just admitted really pained him. His hand comes off my shoulder and rests in his lap. He looks down at his fingers, causing his dark hair to fall over his forehead. He doesn't look back up at me when he says, "I don't know what happened with Connor, but love doesn't destroy."

I sigh, not willing to give him any more of an explanation. I wait for him to look back up at me before I speak. "Love does destroy. It destroys more than anything else in the universe. You're in a perfect world where you have this perfect relationship where love can heal all, but that isn't the case for all of us. Love might complete you, but it destroyed me." I grab my bag from the corner of the booth and turn to him, silently begging him to move.

He lets out a long exhale before he slides out, but he still stands in my way.

I manage to get out and stand, but it forces me to stand right in front of him—our bodies only a mere inch apart. His chest rises quickly and I wonder why my words have this kind of effect on him. I can smell the scent of his cologne, a perfect mix between earthy and sweet. The smell of mint drifts from his mouth, sending my senses into overdrive.

I look him in the eye, bracing myself for whatever cliché saying about love that's about to leave his mouth. He surprises me by not uttering a word. He pins me with an unreadable gaze for a few moments before he pulls his hood up over his face and retreats out the bar.

I'm left staring at his back, wondering why I feel disappointed that, this time, he didn't put up a fight.

20

MAVERICK

I walk through the front door to find Selma waiting for me.

"Where did you go?" She sits on a bar stool at the kitchen counter, her phone laid out in front of her. The look on her face is sad, almost defeated. I want to wipe it off her face.

"I was at Lenny's." My keys make a chiming sound when they fall into the bowl on the table by the door. I take off my coat slowly, hanging it on the hook. The beat of my heart starts to pick up when it seems like we're about to have a conversation I'm not ready for.

I won't lie to Selma. We know each other too well for lies.

"And what was at Lenny's?" She turns her body in the chair, completely facing me. Her short hair is wet, sending droplets of water down her bare shoulders.

I track the movement with my eyes. My mind skips to all the times my lips have traveled that same pathway.

She speaks again, catching my attention. "Or who was at Lenny's?" Those green eyes analyze me while she waits patiently for an answer.

It isn't lost on me that she's never had to question me before. Not like this at least.

And now, she's waiting for an answer I'm afraid to give. An answer I know will put a wedge between us, even though it was never my intention to do so. "Veronica."

She nods, as if she already knew. Her small hand runs through the short-wet strands of her hair, tousling it all. She bites her bottom lip, something she does when she's working through a thought. Her mouth opens to say something, but I speak before she can.

"Selm, it's not like that." I step closer to her, but I know her body language like I know my own, and when she moves deeper into the chair, I can tell she doesn't want me close to her. I feel it in my heart. It aches and squeezes and sends a pit straight to my stomach.

She never backs away from me. Usually she walks straight into my embrace. Something is different between the two of us. I start to realize my innocent friendship with Veronica has added up to something different in her eyes—something worse, something that doesn't *seem* so innocent.

We're both silent, our eyes staring at the other's in the middle of our empty house. The home we built *together* after we both moved out of the dorms after freshman year. We've made so many memories here. Memories that haunt. Memories that are now being tainted by the conversation about to unfold. The only light in the room comes from the dim lights above the stove. My gaze takes in every inch of her, as I try to predict what exactly she's thinking.

"I didn't say it was like anything, Maverick." Her phone vibrates loudly against the granite countertop, but neither of us look at it.

My hand reaches up to rub my chin, feeling the stubble I've been too lazy to shave over the last few days. I know I need to do something instead of just standing here like a dumbass. I try to think of the next thing I should say. For the first time in my life, I feel like I have to justify myself to Selma and it feels weird. It isn't us. It isn't something I've ever had to do.

"My dad called tonight." Those green eyes drift over my face, gauging my reaction. Her head is tilted, waiting for my response.

"I'll talk to him." The words automatically tumble out of my mouth, before I even know what their conversation consisted of this time.

She lets out a long sigh, one that sounds like I've let her down. "That's the thing, Maverick. I've been thinking about this a lot in the last few weeks. Since we were kids, you've been my rock, my home, and I think we've both gotten used to it. I think we've gotten comfortable with it. Too comfortable."

"What's wrong with being comfortable with that, Selm? I want to be there for you when you need me."

She adjusts in her chair and continues her last thought like I hadn't even said anything. "We've gotten so comfortable we haven't even realized that we no longer have a relationship outside of you saving me and me needing saving." A tear runs down her cheek.

I step closer to her again and this time she lets me. I don't touch her, but I cage my arms around her. My body just needs to be close to hers. To feel her proximity.

"What are you even saying, Selm?"

Another tear escapes. I think of all the times I've seen her tears fall, but this is the first time they've ever fallen because of me. Until now, my job has always been to simply wipe them away.

"I'm saying that our relationship is a lie," she states. "We aren't a couple. We're just two best friends that are co-existing, neither one having the courage to mess up what we've always known."

My mouth opens to argue otherwise, to change her mind, but she holds up a hand and says, "Please just let me get this out. I've thought a lot about it recently and I need to tell you every sad thought."

I nod, lowering my head to look at our bodies that are inches apart.

"When I told you my dad called, your first reaction was to fix it for me instead of asking what he said. If you had asked, I would've told you that he and I had a long conversation about our father-daughter relationship. He wants me to come home to visit and talk it out."

"I'm sorry I didn't ask. I'll stay out of it. I love you." The hand that's been resting on the counter between us lifts up and cups her cheek.

She lets me do it, she even leans against it, like she's allowing herself the small comfort. Our eyes are locked as she continues to dump her thoughts on me. "I love you, too, but I think we've been lying to ourselves. I think we're in love with the roles we let the other play. You love being the savior, the rescuer. I love being rescued. But that doesn't mean we're *in* love. I've thought about it all so much. I don't know if I've ever actually been in love with you, Maverick, and it's devastating. We've been together for years. I should be able to say with absolute certainty that I'm in love with you, or that I was at some point, but I can't."

Her hands are flying around all over the place as she talks. She gets so animated about things, and I used to love watching her tell stories with those hands waving around, but now it just hurts to see. Because when she does it, I know she's passionate about what she's talking about. That she's put a lot of thought into it and she means every single word she says. Knowing that, while hearing her words, causes my heart to shatter. Not because I just found out she's never been in love with me, but because she's confirming something I never wanted to acknowledge.

Our relationship has always been a lie—a beautiful lie that neither of us realized we were even telling.

It fucking hurts. It hurts like hell to realize that you've given your all to something, committed to it. But your heart—that pesky little shit—has never followed suit.

Her finger traces over my hand that still cups her cheek. "It hurts me in so many ways to say all this. It feels like I'm chewing glass as I do so. But I have to. It'd be wrong for us to stay in this relationship just because we're comfortable with the circumstances."

"I don't know anything but you, Selm. I'm not ready to give up on this."

"I'm scared that if we stay together, we'll grow to resent each other. You would resent me for chaining you down and I would resent you for fighting all my battles. I can't let that happen to us. I love you so much, Maverick. A part of my heart will always belong to you. We are Selma and Maverick. Destiny. But I think it's time we both realize that our destiny is to be *friends*—just friends. To be there for each other for the rest of time. We can't do that if we're busy living in this charade that we're in a happy, loving relationship. You say you don't want to give up on us, but I think we both gave up on us a long time ago without even noticing it. We both gave up the moment we stopped wanting the absolute best for each other."

I can't help but reach out to her, pulling her as close to me as possible.

I'm mourning a relationship I thought I'd have my whole life. Hindsight is twenty-twenty, and after hearing her out, I understand where she's coming from. Neither of us deserves to be in a relationship that lacks passion, a desperate need for the other person, but I never thought we would end. I thought the love I had for her had always been enough. I see now that you can love somebody with every single part of you—and I mean *every* fucking part of you—yet it doesn't mean you're *in love* with them. I wouldn't have thought that to be true—before—but it *is*.

And it leaves us both in a shattered mess.

She strokes my back as I drag on this moment with her for as long as possible. I hope, with everything I have, that we can both get over this and actually stay friends. That we can stay *Maverick and Selma* without the title of *boyfriend and girlfriend* attached to it. But it's fucking scary because there's no guarantee that we'll be able to pick up where we left off.

And a life without Selma is a life I don't want.

"What if we tried harder?" I ask, a last desperate attempt to keep her.

Her fingers pause. "We can't. I think you've already started to give the part of you away that I never really had. And that's the part of you that matters. The part of you that doesn't feel a responsibility. The part of you that falls hard and fast and wildly. I don't have that part of you. I don't think I ever have, but I think someone else does now. Or could, at least."

I look up at her, emotion lodged deep in my throat. She's talking about Veronica in a way I've never allowed myself to even think of. It's weird to hear these things come from her mouth, because I would have refused to voice any of it for the rest of my life. It's in this moment that I realize I may actually have some sort of feelings for Veronica. I never wanted to acknowledge them, and probably never would have if it weren't for this newfound freedom.

With Selma in my arms, I feel guilty for having this revelation.

I hold onto her for another moment longer before I step back. "I don't want to talk about Veronica. Nothing ever happened between the two of us. Just because I was with her tonight doesn't mean anything."

Selma's fingers swipe underneath her eyes. Her tiny shoulders rise and fall with a deep breath. A thousand different thoughts run through my head. Half of them belong to Selma, the other half to Veronica.

"I *want* to talk about her, Maverick. I know nothing *happened* between the two of you. God, I know that. And honestly, it makes me feel worse, because I know you would've stayed with me forever, even if you were falling for her. You've always felt such a duty to protect me. I hate it. I don't want that kind of love, Maverick. And I don't want that for you. I understand that nothing happened between the two of you, but I won't continue to be the reason that nothing does. I know you love me, but I think you want her. Or could want her. The attraction between you two is obvious to anyone with eyeballs. Always has been."

I shake my head at her. "You don't understand. Nothing will or would ever happen with me and Veronica. The only reason we're even friends is because she never wants a relationship ever again, and because I have—or had—a girlfriend. She looked at me as a safe person to be friends with."

"Maybe something will happen, maybe something won't. But, Mav, you owe it to yourself to have that option. I deserve it, too. Which is partially why I'm leaving you. I'm going to stay with Madison until midterms are over and then I'm going home. For the first time since we were children, I'm going to face my family for real. It might suck. I might completely break down, but it's a breakdown I need to have. I need to learn to fight my own battles, to rescue myself, and you need to learn that love isn't about putting someone else back together, making them whole while you give pieces of yourself away until you have nothing left of yourself. We both have things we need to work out with ourselves, and we need to do that *apart* from each other."

She steps off the barstool. We both stand there, just staring at each other. For the first time, I *feel* the distance between us. It's odd how spoken truths can change everything.

"Do you feel the need to save her?" Selma asks, breaking the silence. Her eyes stay on me until I finally answer.

"No. I feel the need for her to save herself." This is something I finally have to admit—even to myself. It's an odd feeling.

"Good." She walks to the couch and picks up a duffle bag I hadn't even noticed.

I go to take it from her, to offer to carry it, but she shakes her head. I guess this is the beginning of her fighting her own battles.

"I'll always love you, Maverick, but I think the love we owe to each other is just the love of lifelong friendship. This isn't the end of our story, but the start of something new. Something better."

She walks up to me and I pull her into my body for what's probably the last time.

It's bittersweet. It's sad. It's a goodbye.

It's an end.

"Goodbye, Selma. I'll always love you, too."

And with that, she walks out the door and I'm left alone in an empty house, with an even emptier heart.

21

VERONICA

I DIDN'T GO HOME last night. I slept in Tristan's bed instead. I hadn't expected it, but he showed up at Lenny's and one thing led to another. Then, I went to my classes today in yesterday's clothing.

I found myself at another bar tonight, too afraid to go home and face Maverick.

So, instead I found Donte.

I think his name is Donte.

Right now, he's kissing me against the front door. He laughs as he presses his weight against me, making a soft *thud* against the surface.

"Shh," I say against his lips. "You'll wake up my roommates."

He snickers before continuing his assault on my mouth. His hands find the narrow of my hips and he slowly lets them drop until they're tucked into the waistband of my jeans.

"You're so hot. I can't wait to explore every inch of you." His hands drop lower and lower down my jeans until he's cupping my ass.

I moan, leaning into him and shoving my tongue even deeper in his mouth. He lets out a growl low in his throat as he pushes me—harder—this time against the door. This time the sound is louder, but it doesn't quite register through my alcohol-influenced mind.

Just as Donte's hands start to explore my body further, the door swings open.

Unfortunately, that same door is the one we were just leaning against. Donte catches himself on the door frame, but I tumble right into a warm body.

"Shit," I mutter as I try to push off the body I just fell into. Strong hands grip my elbows and spin me and I come face-to-face with Maverick. "Double shit," I mumble.

His blue eyes are ice as they stare intently right over my head. They flick to me quickly, before looking back to the man in the doorway.

"Sorry to wake ya, man," Donte says, extending his hand in what appears to be a fist bump. "We'll be quiet when we go to her room, I think."

Donte winks, and when I look back at Maverick, I notice a slight tick in his jaw as his nostrils flare. Donte looks down at his still outstretched hand, Maverick doing the same.

"She's a stage-five clinger," Maverick lazily drawls when he moves past us, then he slams the door in Donte's face. The reverberation of the door being slammed makes the frames on the wall shake.

I stare in shock at the spot where, just seconds ago, Donte was standing. Now it's just our ugly green door in my view. My gaze zeroes in on Maverick who's staring right back at me. The look on his face breaks me out of my shock.

"What the hell, Maverick!" I yell, running a hand through my hair.

Maverick grabs me by the elbow and pulls me down the stairs to the basement. We pass the pool table and the old junky card table until we're in my room. He closes the door behind us but doesn't let go of my arm.

"Let go of me!" I protest, trying to pull my arm from his grip.

"Are you trying to wake up the whole house?" he accuses, his fingers slowly letting go of me, one by one.

Unfortunately, I can still feel the heat from them even after they're gone.

"You just told him I'm clingy! I most definitely am *not* clingy!" I let out a breath of frustration at his cool demeanor. I swear this guy is never set off.

A small smile pulls at one corner of his mouth. "I had to get rid of him somehow."

"No, you didn't! We were right in the middle of…some unfinished business we needed to attend to," I counter. The alcohol suddenly hits me and I feel the urge to sit down. I take the few steps to my bed and plop down on the white comforter.

"You mean sex?" he asks, but it comes out more like a statement.

"Yes, Maverick, *sex*. Not all of us are in committed relationships like you. We have to get off somehow."

His eyes widen for a fraction of a second before he runs a finger over his lip. He looks like he wants to say something, but he must decide against it because he lets out a long sigh. We both glare at each other.

I sit on my bed, my head starting to spin. He stands across from me, his body leaning against my dresser.

"You're better than being used for sex," he says matter-of-factly.

I don't miss how condescending his tone sounds. It makes my blood boil. He has no place telling me this. I laugh maniacally. "You're such an ass, Maverick. We were going to use *each other* for sex. I wanted to get off, so did he. I had zero expectations from him. I'd rather be *used for sex* than have someone want a relationship out of me."

A crease forms between his dark eyebrows. "Why are you so hell bent on not wanting a relationship?"

He hesitantly walks across the room and takes a seat next to me, so close our arms are touching. It's odd, the way the slight brush of his arm against mine has my senses on overdrive.

"I don't do relationships. I do sex," I say.

"Why won't you do both?" His fingers brush over the ruffles of my comforter. It feels intimate—him, sitting on my bed, running his fingers over the covers I sleep in.

"Because I just can't, Maverick. Now off you go!" I get up, grabbing his arm and pulling to get him off my bed. To get him out of my personal space. I'm reminded just how many tequila shots I took by the way I stumble, causing me to land right against Maverick.

Our bodies are flush. We're eye-to-eye, my chest against his chest.

If he were to look down, he would see that goosebumps are starting to form on my skin. The way I feel right now pisses me off because I don't want to feel this way. I'm close enough to see, when he looks down, that his eyelashes fan over his sharp cheek-bones. I can see that scar, the imperfection that runs down his mouth. The one I can't wait to paint.

His hands are steady as they sit on the small of my waist. They're warm, searing completely through my sweatshirt. "Tell me about Connor."

It feels like a punch to my stomach. I'm not ready for him—for anyone—to look at me the way I see myself. But maybe I need to be.

Because once he knows the truth, he won't look at me the way he seems to be looking at me right now. The way he's never looked at me before. The way a man with a girlfriend shouldn't be looking at another woman. The way a girl like me doesn't even deserved to be looked at.

Am I imagining this?

"I'm afraid," is all I say. It's vulnerable, probably the first time I've allowed myself to be in a long time.

"I'll still be here afterward." His hands tighten on my waist and I can't help it.

I shouldn't.

Dear god, I know I shouldn't.

He has a girlfriend and I actually respect that. Or I thought I did, but this can be added to my list of *Shitty Things Veronica Does in the Name of Being Selfish*, because I lean even closer to him. Our foreheads touch. His breath hits my face every time he breathes out. I wish he would say something—do something—to stop whatever's about to happen, but it's clear he's as lost in this as I am.

My legs shake underneath me. I would love to blame it on the alcohol, but it isn't that. I want to collapse on top of him, crawl inside his body and live in his warmth forever. I'm nervous to look him in the eye, but I do it anyway. Those baby blues are pinned right on me, willing me to say something. Staring into his eyes is like staring into the ocean, and for once, I don't hate it. The way his eyes roam over my face—slowly and with purpose —makes me feel more intoxicated than the liquor I'd downed earlier.

I think over his words to me. I want them to be true. I want him to still look at me *like this* after I tell him the truth. But I know he won't. And I know it's for the best that he won't, but I hold onto the moment for a little while longer.

I pull away from him then—wanting to completely escape his warmth, this feeling—but his hands still rest on the narrow of my waist and it doesn't appear he's willing to move them. I make it so we have no point of contact except his arms on my waist and my thighs touching his as I stand between his legs.

"Connor and I were a love story that was never supposed to happen. We were so different, but somehow it worked. Growing up, I was a brat."

My heart pounds in my chest.

I haven't told this story in years. I barely even spoke of it after it happened. But here I am, wanting to pour out my soul to Maverick.

"I was a spoiled, entitled, rich bitch. I wasn't abnormally mean to others or anything like that, but I was too wrapped up in my own head to care about anyone else. I had a lot of insecurities. Connor called me out on all of it, from the beginning. We were two very different people that came from very different backgrounds, but we met in the middle. Our version of the middle, anyway. It sounds cliché and I want to throw up even saying it, but he made me a better person. Not even just that, but he made me *want* to be a better person. Which was something I never wanted to be until him."

Until now, I've managed to keep eye contact with Maverick, but as we get to the nitty gritty, I'm scared to maintain it. I want to look away when I dump all my baggage at his feet, but I also want to witness his reaction. I want to read every single line of his face to find what might run through his head.

"We were basically a year into our relationship when he died, and it was my fault." I take a shaky breath in. I know Maverick has to feel me trembling beneath his hands. I'm terrified to show him how terrible of a person I actually am, for him to know completely what I did.

"Connor and I had gotten into an argument. I was being young and stupid and petty—basically my typical self, back then. I was convinced he was looking at one of our friends. In my mind, he obviously wanted her and not me. I was so insecure. But more than that, I loved to fight. Fighting with Connor was my favorite thing to do. I was so fucked up in the head that I felt like he showed me *more* love when we were fighting.

"So, even though deep down I knew Connor loved me with everything a seventeen-year-old could give, I dragged out our fight. I'm from a small town on the coast. We were always in the ocean. Our fight happened right in the middle of the crashing waves. I was being a stubborn brat and went into the water and he followed me in. It was deep, and it was night, and we both should've paid attention to the tide. But we were too wrapped up in our teenage relationship angst. He said something that pissed me off, so I lashed back out at him.

"He was so upset with me that he swam away from me, deeper into the ocean. The rest is a blur. I lost him in the water, and by the time I found him and pulled him to shore, he was pronounced dead." I know tears are rolling down my face, but I let them. If I'm going to let Maverick dive into the fucked up abyss that is my mind, he's going to get the emotion that comes with the trauma as well.

"The palms of my hands were bruised from trying to do so many chest compressions on him. I went off the deep end after that. I refused to talk to anyone, including my parents. The only person I even *remotely* talked to was my therapist, and even that was the bare minimum. It took me a year and a half to tell him the whole story. I was so shitty, I didn't even go to Connor's funeral. I was too much of a coward to even look his parents in the eye after what happened. They've reached out over the years, even going as far as staying friends with my parents, but I still can't look at them without wishing *I* was the one who drowned."

My lip trembles. "I was the reason he died, Maverick. *Me.* It was me and my fucked up head that doesn't know how to accept love from others. I don't know anything other than living in my own selfish insecurities. And he died because of it. I didn't hold him underneath the water until his lungs quit, but I might as well have. Because we were in there for the most bullshit of reasons and I can't even look myself in the mirror because of it."

It's silent for so long.

I stare at him as if I have a magnifying glass to his face. Every single tiny movement is one I don't miss.

"So that's why you were glaring at that note the day we first met?" he asks.

What the fuck?

Did he hear anything I just said?

Did he not see the fucking embarrassing tears escaping out of my eyes? And he's asking about a flyer?

All I can do is nod, too confused to do anything else.

He thinks over it for a minute, like he's working everything out in his mind. I try to find what's running through it right now. His hands are still on me, so he can't be completely repulsed by my actions.

But I spoke too soon because his hands lift off my hips then. They stay suspended in the air for a moment. I stare at them, already missing the weight of them against me.

And then he does something that turns my world upside down.

Those large hands go to both of my cheeks and cup them, his fingers curling around the back of my head and landing in my hair. He pulls my face against his. We're forehead to forehead again—our eyes pinned on the other person.

"Veronica, you messed up. You made a mistake—a mistake that had a very large consequence—and I'm sorry. I'm so fucking sorry that happened to you. No one should have to go through that. But it isn't all your fault. We all make decisions that affect others. It's part of life. You made yours and Connor made his. It sounds like Connor's decision was to be in that water, to swim deeper, and it cost him his life. And I hate that that happened to the two of you, I do.

"But you need to learn to forgive yourself for what happened. Because if you truly *were* selfish, you wouldn't carry all this guilt with you, years later. Forgive yourself for the mistake you made. Forgive yourself because you are here and Connor isn't, and even though I know you would've rather been the person to have drowned, you didn't. So all you can do is be a person Connor would have been proud to love. Be that person, Veronica."

At that, I'm a puddle of emotions. My first impulse is to lash out at him, to say something to make him understand that it *is* all my fault, but I don't. Instead, I turn his words over in my head. My eyes close, unable to look at him another moment longer. I'm too overcome. There are too many things happening at once. I want to retreat. I *need* to retreat.

He must see the fear written all over my face because he doesn't stay and pin me down for my answers.

No, he does something worse.

He brings his lips to my forehead and presses those imperfect lips right between my eyebrows.

And then he leaves.

He leaves because he just read me like an open book.

He leaves, and I think a little piece of my messed up heart leaves with him.

22

VERONICA

I PAINT ALL NIGHT. My heart pours out onto the countless canvases I fill.

Green eyes.

Blue eyes.

Eyebrow scars.

Lip scars.

My mind doesn't even keep track of the time. The only things I focus on are my paintbrushes and the canvas. Every feeling overtaking me is added to the canvas. The hate, despair, guilt, loathing, pity, love, want, hope, all painted in many different colors.

The shades of my emotions.

After I run out of paint, I finally step back and look around at them. They're scattered all over my bedroom. It looks like a gallery of my life. Of my obsessions.

Of imperfections.

And for once, mine are included on display. It's odd. I've always been so used to capturing others' imperfections that it never even *occurred* to me to paint my own. But after speaking with Maverick, I felt the impulse to capture my own. To put them on display—as *my* decision, the way *I* wanted them put out there.

I fall asleep long enough to allow the paint to dry. Too

exhausted, emotionally and physically, to even change out of my clothes beforehand that are covered in paint.

When I wake up the next morning, I realize there's paint splattered all over my room. On the walls, the dresser, the door. All over my sheets after I fell asleep with wet paint on my clothing.

I'm too desperate to get to Clementine's gallery to care. I quickly put on new clothes and carry all the canvases I can manage up the stairs and to my car.

I'm busy putting the first load of canvases into my trunk when Maverick runs up the sidewalk. It's apparent he's just coming home from a run. Sweat drips down his forehead, even though the November breeze is frigid.

"What are these?" He pulls a headphone out of his ear, stepping right next to me to peer into my trunk.

Facing up, is a picture I painted of myself. It isn't one that made me go too deep into my emotions. It's of my back. Above my left hip sits a birthmark that's large and two shades darker than the rest of my creamy white complexion. "My paintings. My imperfections."

He isn't even looking at me right now, his eyes taking in every curve of my artwork. Yet it feels more intimate than any other time he's ever looked at me. The way his eyes follow every brushstroke, it makes me squirm.

"Hey, could you help me bring the rest up?" I ask him. I can't believe I'm about to let him see what I painted—to see that I painted *him*. Maybe I'm just too burnt out to care.

All I need right now is to get these paintings—these imperfections—out into the world. Which means I need to get them to Clementine's right this moment.

He nods, gesturing for me to lead the way.

We're silent as we walk through the house and into the basement. It briefly occurs to me that I haven't seen Aspen or Selma in days.

When we enter my room, Maverick abruptly stops. His eyes dart around the room like he doesn't know where to look first. I don't blame him, there's a lot to look at.

I'm allowing him into my life on a whole new level. My

words are one thing, but my art is something completely different. And the way he's looking at my art—like fucking Picasso did it, not me—makes my toes curl in my boots.

I watch him stare at the piece that is so obviously him. It's a profile of his face, the side that features the scar down his lips.

At first, I just wanted to paint his lips—the lips that I dreamed of having on me last night, even though he very much has a girlfriend—but it felt too intimate.

In the painting, his jawline is sharp. Those blue eyes brought to life in oil paints stare back at you the same way Maverick does, like he's busy figuring you out.

"Veronica," he says, looking at me, his hand over his chest. "I don't even know what to say. These are—"

"Don't say anything," I say, picking up the closest canvas to me. I wrap my arms around it and turn to face him. "Please, just —nothing. I can't even believe I'm letting you see these. I just need help taking them to my car and getting them out of the house."

It must take some time for him to process what I said, but I give him credit for leaving it at that. Instead of saying anything else, he helps me gather the rest of the canvases and bring them to my car.

Just when I'm about to slam the trunk shut, he reaches in and pulls a canvas from the top. It's the one I painted of myself. My most vulnerable one.

In the painting, I'm staring at something in the distance. My hands encompass both sides of my face, the way he did last night, and tears run down my face. My shoulders cave in, the invisible guilt weighing me down. All the edges are smeared and run down the canvas in a trail of emotions.

It showcases everything I've ever felt.

And I never want to see it again.

It was a cathartic experience meant to only be that— cathartic and then forgotten.

"I'm keeping this," Maverick says, wrapping it in his hands like it's the most precious item he's ever owned. I want to argue with him that he has no right to snatch it, but before I can, he's already walking toward the house.

He doesn't even look back at me. He just leaves me alone with my thoughts for the second time in twenty-four hours.

WHEN I DROP the canvases off at Clementine's, she cries. Only because I've never brought these many paintings in at once and because I tell her to sell them all, under a name that's not my own. I drop them off with her and leave, unable to think about who might buy them. I can't think about the fact that they won't know that every part of my grief is attached to the different colored brushstrokes.

I can't think about any of it.

23

VERONICA

"YOU CONSIDER US FRIENDS, RIGHT?" Aspen asks as he barrels into my room, two days after I dropped my paintings off at Clementine's.

I look up from my laptop, my fingers pausing on the keyboard while I take a look at the man in my doorway. "Excuse me, what?"

Aspen rolls his eyes, his hand lifting to rub at the buzzed hair on his head. "We're friends, right?"

My lips purse as I think over his words. If anyone asked me when I first moved in here if Aspen and I could ever be friends, I would have laughed in their face. He's exactly the kind of guy I would purposely ignore. He comes off as a complete douchebag, but I knew from the beginning that underneath all the playboy antics, he had a golden retriever heart. Loyal to a fault. The need to be loved.

All the other mushy gushy stuff, I still want no part in. But the guy has weaseled his way into my heart, little by little. I'm stunned to realize I actually might consider him a *friend*.

As I'm thinking it through, he walks into my room and plops down on the foot of my bed. He cradles his head in his hands, releasing a long breath. "I mean I know you have this whole *don't fuck with me attitude* about you, V. But I was kind of thinking that you and I might be friends, and I need a friend right now—

like right fucking now." There's strain in his voice as he talks to the floor, staring at his perfectly clean loafers.

Aspen peeks out at me from beneath his fingers, and in his eyes, I see something I'm not expecting.

Fear.

I could recognize that look in anybody's eyes. Because it's a look I've found on myself in the mirror for many years now.

I know what I'm afraid of.

But what is *Aspen* afraid of?

Even though my feelings are all over the place—like the splatters of my paint—I decide to let Aspen splatter the canvas a little more with whatever he's dealing with.

As soon as I place my laptop on my nightstand, Aspen turns around to look at me.

"I guess we are friends," I say.

He gives me a haphazard smile, picking a piece of lint off his chino pants. "Okay, then as my friend, I really need your advice on something."

"Why can't you talk to Maverick about it?" I ask him.

His eyes widen for a split second. The muscles underneath his T-shirt tense at my words. Aspen sucks in through his teeth and says, "This isn't exactly a conversation I can have with Maverick." His eyes find mine and then it all clicks together.

Oh.

I nod as I sit up in bed, my shoulders resting against my tufted headboard. I try to pull the comforter up to my shoulders, but it's stuck underneath his body. "Take off your shoes."

"Veronica, I need you to not pay attention to my *shoes*. I need you to listen to me before I lose my shit. I—"

"Fucking listen for once in your life, Aspen. Take off your shoes and get your ass off my comforter so I can pull it up. Then come sit here." I flip the comforter over in the empty spot next to me, inviting him in.

I'm willingly letting Aspen in my bed. Who would've guessed?

But by the look in his eyes, I know this is something serious. Something to do with a girl. And for some reason, I want to be there for him.

I wait as Aspen slides those hideous loafers off and crawls

into my bed. His head bumps against my headboard as he gets comfortable, his body stretching out across the side he's on.

For a minute, he and I just sit there. Both of us underneath my white comforter, staring at the mirror across from us.

We aren't touching at all, but I can feel his presence next to me. It's oddly comforting. To know I have a man in my bed and there aren't any expectations—just friends. I want to be a good friend to him, now that I've realized his heart is taken. I don't think *he's* realized it, but it's pretty obvious.

Now the only question is: What she will do with it?

"So, who's the girl?" I ask, turning my head to look at him.

His head whips to the side, facing me. "I can't tell you."

I nod, not looking away from him. I'm fairly confident I know who's putting his heart through the wringer right now, but I won't butt into his business. If he wants to tell me who it is, he will.

"I can tell you, though, that I think I have it bad," he says. "Like, *really* fucking bad, Veronica." He groans as he stretches his long legs underneath the comforter. His body inches down the headboard until his buzzed head rests against my pillow, and he folds his hands over his stomach.

"Does she know this?" I stare at the way he twiddles his thumbs around and around.

"No. She thinks I hate her. Or at least that I'm repulsed by her. But in reality, I haven't slept with another girl in ages. Because when my lips touch another girl's, *her* damn face pops into my head."

I contemplate what he's saying. "Well, do you plan on telling her that?"

"No. The thing is, we would never work. It'd be too complicated, and it'd hurt somebody else in my life. I can't do it. But I want to do it. How is that even possible?"

Maverick's face flashes in my mind—along with the feelings for him that have started to spin around in my heart and in my head. Feelings I shouldn't be having. Because we can't be anything. I know that. But it doesn't mean I don't want it.

"Are you sure it would hurt somebody else?" I ask him. I

think of Selma, feeling guilty for wanting something from a man who has a perfect relationship with a perfect girl.

She's perfect. I'm nothing but imperfections. If it were up to him, who would he choose?

As soon as the thought enters my mind, I rub my eyes, trying to force it out. My selfish heart is doing what it does best—wanting what it wants, consequences be damned.

But I won't pursue that. I will continue to force down the feelings I'm starting to develop for a man I swore I would stay *just friends* with.

The shifting of Aspen's body brings me back into the present with him. "I'm *sure* it would hurt somebody else. I know it'd hurt everybody involved. But that doesn't make it hurt any less now, and it doesn't make me want her any less. I'm starting to realize that maybe—maybe I've wanted this for years."

I mimic his movements from earlier, sliding down the headboard and resting my head against the pillow. My hands reach out and pull at the ponytail that's holding my hair up, the position of my head on the pillow making it uncomfortable to lie on.

"I think you should tell her."

Aspen gasps next to me. "Are you not listening to me at all? I can't tell her, that's the problem. I don't think I want anyone but her, but I can't have her. So now I'm stuck going crazy. And I'm horny."

I laugh. "I don't know what else to tell you then, bud. Either you tell her—or show her—how you feel, or you need to move on and find somebody else. But I can guarantee you that if you stay in this limbo you're in right now, it won't do anything but continue to drive you crazy."

Look at me giving advice. Damn, maybe I can be a good friend.

"You suck at this, V."

My eyes dart to him. "All I'm doing is pointing out something you already know."

His hands slide over his face, pulling at the skin on his cheeks. "You're right. I need to forget about her. They're just silly feelings. They'll go away."

I flip over to look at him. This is not going in the direction I was hoping it would. I was thinking with a little tough love, he'd be pushed in her direction. My thought process was that maybe he would grow a pair and go for it.

But apparently Aspen has other plans.

Just as I'm about to ask him if he's sure, a soft knock interrupts my thoughts. I lift my head from the pillow to find Maverick in the doorway. His eyes roam around the bed—the bed in which Aspen and I lie—where it may appear a little less innocent than it actually is.

"Oh hey, Mav," Aspen says, propping himself up on his elbows. The movement causes the comforter to slip off the both of us. Aspen's eyes follow its path, his gaze stuck on the pool of white on my carpet.

Maverick's still staring intensely at the comforter on the floor when Aspen says, "What do you guys think about throwing a party tonight?"

This catches Maverick's attention, his eyes traveling to where Aspen has fully sat up in my bed.

I follow Aspen's lead, pulling my legs up to my chest. My chin rests on my knees while I stare at Maverick who clears his throat, his eyes looking over at me now. The look he gives me is intense. I wish I knew what the meaning behind it was, but it probably wouldn't help things.

"I think a party sounds great," I tell Aspen, breaking away from Maverick's intense gaze.

Aspen looks over at me with a sly grin on his face. "Really?"

"Let's do it," I decide.

24

MAVERICK

I HATE that I can't get the image of my best friend in Veronica's bed out of my head.

It's been hours—a party now in full swing at our house—but I'm sitting in the basement in a corner where I can somehow still be alone, thinking of the way Veronica and Aspen had been cozy in her bed.

The logical part of me knows there's absolutely nothing going on between them. But there's another part of me that feels nothing but jealousy when I think back to the sight.

I'd originally gone downstairs to tell Veronica that Selma and I were over. The guilt from keeping that information a secret was just eating away at me.

I had zero expectations on how Veronica might react to the news. I didn't want to tell her because I thought something would happen between the two of us. I wanted to tell her just so it would be out in the open. And so she heard it from *me*.

But instead, I found her and Aspen in deep conversation. Both of them underneath her blanket, their bodies only a few inches apart.

I didn't know if I was more jealous of *Aspen* being in her bed or that she may have been telling things to him that she hadn't told me.

My heart didn't want her to tell secrets to anybody *but* me. I wanted to keep all her secrets like they were my own. I wanted to lock them deep inside my heart, to relish in the fact that she trusted them with me and no one else.

I hadn't thought of how I might feel if her secrets were being told to another.

I'm still trying to work through my feelings when Veronica's body appears and sits down next to mine.

"Aspen sure knows how to throw a party." She looks around the crowded space while I look at her.

Her blue eyes are lined in black, making them even more striking. She has her long blonde hair perfectly curled. Currently, it falls down her back, reaching all the way down her spine. She's wearing some kind of shirt that's basically see-through, something I haven't been able to miss as I've watched her drift around the party all night.

When she first walked out of her room in that outfit earlier, I was thankful there weren't many people around to see my reaction. Or my lack thereof, rather, because the sight of her had pinned me to my spot. I'd been listening to Aspen rattle on about all the people he invited when her door opened.

She stepped out in a pair of black jeans that molded to every inch of those lean legs of hers. The sight of her made my stomach clench. It literally hurt to look at her because I was starting to come to terms with how much I wanted her.

The top of her was wrapped in some kind of mesh fabric that barely attempted to cover the skin underneath. Anybody who looked at her could see right through it, all her skin exposed except for the small amount hidden beneath her black bra.

She finished it off with a pair of pink combat boots. Veronica stomped around in that little bit of color in an otherwise all-black outfit. It was so like her.

A contradiction.

A contradiction I'm slowly becoming obsessed with.

Now, a pair of hot pink fingernails snaps in front of my face. "Earth to Maverick." Veronica draws her hand back to her side, but she leans closer to me, trying to catch my attention.

"Sorry," I respond, looking around at the party before looking back at her.

"Yeah, well, if one more person attempts to go into my room to hook up, I might cut them." She stares across the basement at her bedroom door.

The party's been going for hours now, and we've reached the point of the night where people have started to pair off, searching for an empty space to continue to get to know each other.

I can't help but smirk when I envision a *very* pissed off Veronica chasing down a couple who were just trying to get it in.

She bumps me with her shoulder. "So, where's Selma tonight?" Her voice is thoughtful, and when I look in her eyes, there's something there that makes my throat feel odd.

I want to tell her that Selma and I are done—over. But I don't want to do it in front of a bunch of horny twenty-somethings. It feels like something that should be admitted in private. Even though Selma and I are no longer together, I'm not sure my heart is ready to jump into something new, especially with Veronica.

Because if my heart goes all in with her, and it doesn't get reciprocated, I'm not sure I'd ever be able to recover from it.

I'm not sure I'm ready for her to hold something I now realize I've never actually given away. I don't have it in me to watch her take those pink combat boots to my heart and stomp all over it.

Because even though I wish it wasn't true, a small part of me knows if I allow myself to fall for her, there's a large chance she won't give a damn.

So, I keep those words in my head, responding another way to her. "She went back home to see her parents." It's not a lie—Selma should be back home with her parents by now, or at least close to it. It's just not the full truth.

"Spin the bottle time!" Aspen cheers from across the basement while moving our coffee table from in front of the couch.

"Is he serious?" Veronica asks, her shoulder lightly brushing against mine.

We're sitting on the other side of the basement, both of us perched on barstools placed against the wall. This was my private corner for most of the night—my place to wallow in my own thoughts—before Veronica had joined me.

"He's probably serious," I respond.

Her eyes are focused on Aspen as he hustles all the stragglers in the basement to join him in the juvenile game. People are humoring him, though, because they all start to sit in a circle in the open space in front of our couches.

Veronica watches him for an extended amount of time until she finally looks at me. We stay like that for a few moments as the party bustles around us. Aspen continues to pester people to play the game, but I barely hear him because I'm too busy peering into Veronica's sad blue eyes.

I wish she would lower her walls a little more—let me into that beautiful mind of hers to see what she thinks when she looks at me like this—but she doesn't.

And neither do I.

I try to hide the way my heart has picked up in my chest. The way I feel in this hollow pit in my stomach when I look at her and stop myself from touching her. I hide the fact that the way she rubs her lips together when she's deep in thought— something she's doing right now—makes blood pump all the way down to my dick.

I hide all of it.

I'm staring at her lips when she speaks. "Oh, fuck it," she says, her gaze flicking to my lips—the lips she painted so vividly like she'd spent her life studying them—before she slides off the barstool and walks over to join Aspen's circle.

I don't register what she's doing until she sits down next to Tristan, giving him a smile that makes me jealous all over again.

Is she really about to play spin the bottle?

She confirms my suspicions when she folds those legs underneath her, her knee bumping against his.

I'm busy staring at their contact when Aspen steps next to me. I think back to the other night, when I finally told my best friend what was going on. After Selma had been gone for a few days, he finally asked me if something happened.

I broke down and told him everything.

I wish I could say he was shocked to hear that Selma and I

hadn't ever really been in love, but he wasn't. It appears that Selma and I were the only two people who'd ever fallen for the charade to begin with.

And maybe Veronica.

Even Lily has called me out on it all.

"I know you love her, man," Aspen had told me during the conversation, his hand running over his buzzed hair. He'd been a few beers in but was somehow still philosophical. "There's no denying it, but I think you need to rethink your definition of being in love. Love isn't about loving someone so much you let nothing break them, it's about loving them even though something has already broken them. That's what you need. That's what Selma needs, too." He said those words and then walked to his room, as if he hadn't sent my head spinning.

I thought love was about *protecting* someone, so they didn't ever have to break at all. But I'm continuously learning that I apparently know *very little* about love.

I do know *one* thing, however.

Veronica.

The girl who's now perched next to another man, about to play a game where I could very well watch her make-out with another guy.

Will I be okay with it?

Probably not.

She hasn't left my head. No matter how many times I've tried—and continue to try—to force her out.

I just got out of a relationship that took up *years* of my life— one I would've stayed in for the rest of it. I shouldn't be thinking of a woman I have to rip truths out of.

Yet, in every spare moment, her haunted gaze finds a way to fill my brain.

The way she'd been vulnerable enough to cry in front of me, to completely fall apart.

How she shared her story with me.

The way she painted herself.

How she painted me, in such vivid detail it felt like I was looking in a mirror.

And I'll be damned if I couldn't forget the way her body felt against mine. The way her lips were no more than an inch away from my own, how the only thing that went through my head was the need to kiss her.

I felt the need to kiss her until she forgot how much she hated herself.

But our lips never touched.

They haven't touched because I don't think either one of us are ready for that.

Before I kiss her, I need to know I run rampant through her mind like she runs through mine. I need to know if, when she goes to bed at night, she's wondering about me.

I need to tell her I no longer have a girlfriend, but it feels so *cheap* to announce that to her. To make it seem like Selma was just some barrier between the two of us, and now that she's gone, we should be something.

I don't even know what I want at this point—the breakup with Selma too fresh.

But I do know I'm too hyperaware of the space Veronica and I share. Even though we have classes together, I've barely said three words to her recently. We may live in the same house, but she's also been avoiding me like the plague.

Aside from barely having any interactions together lately, I'm still too aware of her.

Her scent lingers in the kitchen after she's been in it.

My mind wanders with thoughts that make my blood rush south when the basement shower runs for thirty minutes straight.

As we sat through the most recent and boring lectures from our professor, she doodled on her notepad, and all I wanted to do was snatch it away from her again and see what she was creating.

I wished it was me.

I hoped she couldn't get me out of her head either and that it reflected in her art.

But there's no way for me to know that or not, because she hasn't allowed me close enough to her to find out.

The few words we've exchanged tonight are already more

than all the ones we've exchanged since the night she confessed everything to me.

I'd told myself I'd give her the space that she needed—especially after she divulged so much of her fucked up past to me—but that doesn't mean it hasn't sucked staying true to my own promise.

When I had watched her hand roam wildly over the piece of paper during class, it made me think of the painting that was stashed under my bed.

The painting that, every night, I pull out and gaze at, as if it might tell me one of her secrets.

But no matter how long I've studied it, I haven't been able to figure her out more.

A cough interrupts me now. And then, "How long are you going to stare at her before you go over there?"

I completely forgot that Aspen was next to me.

"Tristan isn't all that bad," he says. "Maybe he'll be good for her."

I turn my head to glare at Aspen, not missing the smug look on his face while he smirks at me. "Shut up," I respond before I resume staring a hole into the back of Veronica's head.

"She's definitely fucked up," Aspen says, "but aren't we all? How could she not be after what she's gone through?" He's watching Veronica now, too.

It feels like someone has an iron fist around my heart when it registers there's a possibility she *also* told Aspen about her past.

I'm too obsessed with her truths. It shouldn't bother me if she's telling them to Aspen too, but here I am, jealous at just the idea of it.

I'm wallowing as he continues with, "She's a good person, though. I like her, even when she's a brat. And I haven't missed how you're looking at her tonight. I've never seen you look at someone like this before, Mav. Just want to make you aware." He stands next to me for a little bit longer before he plasters that panty-dropping smile on his face and walks over to the circle.

I'm about to retreat to my room for the night, my body now at the foot of the stairs. I'm so close to leaving. But when I look over my shoulder and find Tristan whispering something in Veronica's ear, I change my mind.

I close the distance to the circle and sit in an empty space next to my sister. Lily's too busy glaring at somebody opposite us to even notice me, which is fine because I'm also staring across the circle, undoubtedly wearing a matching glare on my own face.

25

VERONICA

When I look up from my conversation with Tristan, I'm shocked to find Maverick sitting across the circle from me.

A circle for spin the bottle.

A circle for a game that involves kissing someone if the bottle lands on you.

A circle for a game that someone in a relationship shouldn't be playing.

Even though he mentioned that Selma was out of town, I scan the circle to see if maybe she's actually here and both of them are playing. Which, now that I think about it, might be a weird kink for the two of them.

Except I don't see Selma anywhere.

It doesn't make sense at all. Maverick's never been anything but respectful, committed, *loyal*.

I leave Tristan mid-sentence. He's explaining something about baseball and how to find the perfect glove when I vacate my spot. My legs take me the short amount of space around the circle before I crouch behind Maverick.

"What the hell are you doing?" I hiss, my lips close to Maverick's ear so nobody can hear our conversation. I don't know how Lily hasn't already kicked her brother in the balls for playing this game when he's dating her *best friend*.

Even though Lily seems distracted tonight, I know how

protective she is over those she cares about. There's no way she'd let Maverick play this game while in a relationship with Selma.

None of it makes sense.

"I'm sitting," Maverick responds, angling his head toward me a bit. Even though it's the smallest amount, it causes our lips to near.

"No shit, Sherlock. I mean what are you doing playing spin the bottle?" My calves start to burn from the crouching position, my hand finding the floor to help steady myself.

"Didn't think you noticed. You were too deep in your conversation with Tristan." Maverick looks at me from the corner of his eyes, his comment stunning me for a moment.

"That has nothing to do with this," I say.

He laughs, the air from it brushing my cheek. The muscle on the side of his jaw tightens as he grinds his teeth together. "Oh, if only you knew that it has *everything* to do with this."

I try to make sense of his words before I remember to get back on topic. "What about Selma?"

Maverick turns his shoulders until he's facing me. Our faces are only a few inches apart, the rest of the party disappearing as he looks at me with a serious gaze. "Selma and I broke up."

The admission causes me to sit back on my knees. It's the last thing I expected to hear from his mouth. It hits me everywhere in my body. It feels like a relief. "Wait, what the fuck?"

His ocean gaze flicks to my mouth before he meets my eyes again. "We broke up. I wanted to tell you, it just didn't feel right. But we're done. She and I will remain friends, as we always should have been."

I can't form words, my head is too busy spinning.

They were supposed to be this perfect couple. *The* perfect couple. They finished each other's sentences, for fuck's sake.

How could they break up?

And why am I happy about it?

Why does it feel like something has just been lifted off my chest to know someone else isn't sharing his bed? Or more importantly, sharing his head.

He doesn't say anything else.

It's an odd feeling to know something that used to be unattainable is now within your reach.

Will I still want him now that I know he's emotionally available?

I'm scared to find out the answer.

Somebody taps me on the shoulder, and I look over to find Lily leaning toward us.

"Hey, you two, I can feel the intensity of your conversation —like can *really* feel it—but the rest of us are trying to play a game." Her hair cascades off her shoulder as she scolds us. There's something written in her eyes that I can't quite read, but just as soon as she looks at us, she's back to glaring at someone across the circle.

My eyes follow in that same direction to find hers pinned on Aspen.

I feel the heat in my cheeks when I continue to look around the circle, realizing that the conversation between me and Maverick wasn't as private as I thought. While I'm confident no one could *hear* what was being said, I do know some were watching it unfold.

With so many things looming in the air, and so many unspoken words, I look at Maverick one last time before I get back up and return to my spot next to Tristan.

"Everything okay?" Tristan whispers next to me, his eyes on Maverick.

I look at Tristan, giving him a nod and what I hope is a convincing smile. Because inside, I'm losing my shit. Part of me wants to jump Maverick's bones, have sex with him until he no longer takes up space in my mind. The other part of me wants to run for the hills because I don't want to put him in the same position as Connor.

Aspen finally takes a spot in the circle after kissing the girl he'd been talking to on the cheek. He places an empty bottle of vodka in the middle of us all. "Tristan, you go first since it's your birthday."

My eyes dart to the man next to me. I didn't know it was his birthday, even after talking to him most of the night.

He looks at me, winking. "Maybe it'll land on you." Then, he reaches for the bottle and gives it a good twirl.

Thank god, it doesn't land on me.

It lands on a red head—a few spots down from Lily—who squeals before eagerly popping her lips together in anticipation. Tristan crawls over to her, planting a kiss against her lips.

I can tell the red head is disappointed when he pulls away a few seconds later. He returns to his spot beside me and the game continues on. Luckily, it's not my turn, as it was decided that the rule of the game would be that the person the bottle landed on would spin next.

As the game plays on, I sneak glances in Maverick's direction. I'm still not over the news he shared with me. It's hard to process. I thought he and Selma had such a solid relationship.

I need to know who ended it.

Why it ended.

I need to know every fucking detail.

I'm staring at the spinning bottle when I realize there's a chance that bottle might land on Maverick. The person sitting next to him kisses somebody just a few spots down from them, which only reinforces the possibility and I don't know how I feel about it.

I'm too busy focusing on the pit in my stomach to look back at Maverick. I'm embarrassed by my reaction to the idea of him possibly kissing another girl. I can't look at him. I can't risk him looking in my eyes and knowing what's going on in my head.

If anyone can read me like an open book, it's Maverick. So, I don't give him the chance to. My eyes are trained on Lily as she leans forward to spin the bottle. Her fingers are just starting to spread around the base when Aspen jumps up from his spot in the circle.

"Hey, Lily, can I talk to you for a second?" he asks.

Lily's eyebrows raise, clearly as shocked by Aspen's interruption as I am. She looks down at the bottle and then back up at Aspen a few times. Finally, she nods her head in confusion, taking her hand off the bottle.

Aspen's shoulders drop in relief.

He's got it bad.

The two of them look at each other oddly as they go start a conversation at the base of the stairs. Everyone in the circle talks amongst themselves for a few minutes before the guy sitting next to Lily's empty spot starts the game back up.

I want to get up and hide in my room, but I also feel this strange need to make Maverick jealous, which is comical because I don't even know if it's possible. I don't know if watching my lips press against another man's would give him the same unease that I felt just *imagining* his against someone else's.

Just as the person next to me goes to spin the bottle, Lily and Aspen both join the circle again. Lily is trying to mouth something to me from across the circle, but apparently, I suck at reading lips.

Whatever their conversation was about, Aspen doesn't seem happy with it. Because when I look at him, there's tension in his shoulders. He stares at his hands, his thumbs circling around each other in his lap.

Tristan puts his warm hand on my leg, making me jump. "Whoa, sorry. Just wanted to see if you were okay," he says.

I look at him for a brief moment, nodding my head. I don't retreat to my room.

"Maverick, why don't you go?" a blonde suggests from across the circle.

I don't miss the flirtatious tone her voice takes on. I feel the need to cross the fucking circle and throttle her. It's not even his turn. The rules were *clearly* stated and it's not his turn.

No fucking thanks.

Next joke, please.

I'm an internal fucking mess when Maverick gets to his knees.

Why in the hell is he getting on his knees?

Is he listening to her?

Is he going to kiss her?

His long tan arm—the one I've caught myself staring at in class because of the interesting way his muscles move as he writes—reaches into the center of the circle and gives the bottle a spin. My gaze is locked on that fucking thing, even as it whirls around and around.

It seems like it spins for an eternity.

I cannot believe I'm hoping it lands on me—the only outcome that might calm the rage in me right now.

If it lands on the cute blonde with the *awful* and obvious suggestion, I will lose my shit in front of all these strangers.

It spins and spins and spins.

My eyes glance up from the bottle to find Maverick staring directly at me.

The look on his face I can easily read.

It looks like *want*, like need—and it's aimed right at me.

A gasp next to me causes me to look back down at the bottle; it's that same moment I notice he's abruptly stopped it with his hand.

Time goes by agonizingly slowly as he turns the bottle until it points to me.

My throat starts to close up as I look over at Maverick, his gaze still trained on me.

It seems that in *this* exact moment, every single person around us has decided it would be a *perfect* time to shut the fuck up. Which sucks, because right now, the silence is deafening. And I'm not ready for what could happen next.

"To hell with this game," he states. "I only want to kiss one person here."

Shut the motherfucking front door.

I can't look away from him. A certain intensity—*or is it intent?*—is all over his face.

"Veronica, it's you," he says, looking at me.

My heart plummets.

It's resting at my freaking feet with the sudden turn of events.

Fucking Maverick.

He just had to go and draw a very clear line in the sand.

Just when I'm about to make some kind of excuse to get my ass out of this situation, I look up to find him inches away from me. Emotion shows in the crease of his brow, in his unwavering gaze, in the way his lips are slightly parted.

I can't kiss him.

His lips can't touch mine. I'm too afraid of what my broken heart will feel afterward.

But I'm not quick enough.

Before I know it, Maverick's fingers are wrapped around my chin. They are strong against my skin as he slowly tilts my head up.

He keeps gently pulling until I'm looking at him, his face only an inch away from mine.

I go to sit back on my heels, my knees pressing into the hard basement floor. His body travels with me, though, and now he's leaning over me, blocking everyone else out from the party.

We stare at each other.

His pointer finger rests right against the pulse in my neck— the racing pulse that's currently giving away all my secrets.

I'm staring at the scar on his lips when his mouth begins to move.

"I don't think I can come back from this, Veronica," he tells me.

"Then don't do it," I warn, trying like hell to avoid this chain reaction that will only end in despair.

"I don't think I can do that either," he murmurs, his voice breaking at the end.

He pulls my lips against his so fast I don't even have time to process it.

It's terrifying.

It's magnetic.

But most of all, it's tragic. Because I can't let it happen again.

Maverick doesn't waste a second, his tongue skirting against my bottom lip. His other hand finds the other side of my face at the same time I open my mouth to him. His hands are clammy against the side of my face, the warmth sending shivers down my body.

Our tongues move against each other so achingly slowly. I feel it everywhere in my body.

Maverick kisses me and it feels like a poem—short, sweet, and with rhythm.

Every inch of my body tingles from the way his lips move against mine.

But most of all, I feel it in my heart.

"Veronica," he whispers against my lips, both of us lost to the people surrounding us.

The way he says my name, it breaks me out of our moment.

Because Maverick says my name like he needs me.

I can't be needed. Not ever again.

I place my hand on his chest, feeling his racing heart beneath his shirt. Our foreheads press against each other in a painstakingly long moment before I do what I have to do. I look him in the eye, focusing for a short moment on his swollen lips.

"I can't do this." I pull his hands from the sides of my face, the warmth from them lingering long after I lock myself in my room.

IT'S BEEN HOURS, and I can still hear voices outside my door. I hear them because I can't sleep.

I can't sleep because I can't forget the way Maverick's lips against mine opened something within me.

My heavily guarded heart has been spilling out, spilling out onto a canvas.

A canvas no one will ever see, but a canvas of our lips pressed together—water colors exploding all around it.

26

MAVERICK

IT'S BEEN days since I've seen Veronica. Ever since our kiss, she's been completely ignoring me. I've gone down to the basement several times to try to speak with her, but my knocks have been ignored.

She's not hiding the fact that she's in her room, making it obvious that it's *me* she's ignoring.

I shouldn't have kissed her during that game; I knew it would start us down a path we couldn't go back from. But there was nothing that could have stopped me from finally tasting her lips for the first time once I had the opportunity. I'd been thinking about her lips longer than I care to admit, and once they were in front of me, I had to take what I wanted.

The kiss; it was excruciating.

Because I knew as soon as her lips met mine that I would want to taste them forever.

And she's made it very clear she has no intentions to keep *anything* forever.

At this point, I would settle for her just to look at me. To talk to me. To do anything with me, even if it doesn't involve our lips meeting.

I miss her snarky comments.

I miss her pink boots.

I miss the way her eyes narrow as she's thinking something through.

I just miss her.

I might be approaching borderline stalker status because I sit on the stairs in the basement, waiting her out while all these thoughts run through my head.

I planned on giving her space, on giving her whatever she needed to process the kiss between the two of us. But a man can only be so patient before he needs to take matters into his own hands.

Hence, me waiting on the stairs like a damn stalker. Because eventually she has to come out of her room.

Right?

Plus, is it truly stalking if it's waiting for someone in your own house?

I like to believe that it isn't.

I find myself aimlessly scrolling through my Instagram feed, something I never check, when Veronica's door finally opens.

She's mid-step out of her room when she looks up and notices me. Her whole body stops. Neither one of us says anything. I slide my phone back into my pocket and stand up.

I make sure to do it slowly, because the look on her face reminds me of a scared animal. I'm afraid that if I move too fast, she'll run.

Once I'm standing, I take a deep breath. "Hi."

"Why are you down here?" Veronica props an elbow against the doorframe, crossing her arms over the pink dress she's wearing.

"Waiting for you," I reply, wanting to take a step closer to her just before I decide against it.

"Waiting for me," she repeats.

I dry my palms on the front of my pants, rubbing them over my thighs. Her eyes follow my movements. "Yes, I want to take you somewhere." I scratch at my head, suddenly anxious.

"You want to take *me* somewhere?"

"I want to take you somewhere." My foot takes the smallest step toward her. We're still separated by a large section of the basement, but it's still progress considering she hasn't run away yet.

"I can't, Maverick." The toe of her boot scrapes at the worn carpet below it. She stares at it for a few moments before she looks at me, a determined look on her face.

I start with, "Look, about the other night…"

I want to tell her it was perfect, that I haven't been able to get it out of my head.

I want to confess to her every thought that has come to my mind since I first *met* her, but I'm not ready for her to shoot me down. I need to take this slow, because at this point, I'll take her in any way I can have her—even if it's in small and fractured increments.

"I don't want to talk about the other night. It was a mistake," she says.

Damn.

Well, that felt like a punch to the gut. A blow I wasn't expecting.

It didn't hurt my ego, though; it hurt my heart.

But I've been reminding myself that I've always known of her aversion to relationships. The entire time I've known her. It's my fault for expecting anything more from her.

So, I won't.

I won't hope for anything more.

I'll take what she will give me and I will fucking *feast* on it.

And right now, I'm hoping she'll just humor me.

"Then let's not talk about it," I say.

I can tell my words shock her by the way she purses her lips. The tiniest line forms on her forehead as she thinks my answer through.

Veronica timidly takes a few steps into the basement living area. A few steps closer to me. "You promise we won't talk about it?" She keeps walking until the toes of her boots are only a few inches away from my sneakers.

I can feel my heart start to race inside my chest. I try not to look too deeply into the fact that Selma never made my heart race like this. But I can't get my hopes up here. Veronica has made it clear where she stands. I have to respect that, even if she's making me feel things I haven't felt before.

"I promise," I respond, reaching my arm between us and holding out a pinky.

She stares at it for a moment. A long moment where I stand in front of her, my pinky outstretched, both of us staring at it between our bodies.

Veronica lifts her hand, gently wrapping her pinky around mine. Just as soon as she does it, she goes to remove it before I stop her.

"Wait, you have to bite it," I remind her.

"What the hell are you talking about?" Her head tilts up, curiosity on her face.

Our pinkies are still wound around the other's.

"You have to bite your thumb to make it legit. Watch." I bend down, opening my mouth and biting softly down on my thumb. I look at her, waiting for her to do the same.

"I think you're making this up," Veronica says before using her free hand to hold her hair against her shoulder.

She stretches up on her toes and wraps that soft mouth around her thumb. I stare at the way her red lipstick leaves lip prints in a ring around the tip of her finger.

Both our hands fall to our sides as we end the promise.

"No, ask Lily. She and I took the thumb bite promise *very* seriously," I insist.

Veronica shakes her head at me, tucking a strand of hair behind her ear. "Where do you want to take me?"

The question comes from her, and it takes me a little off guard. I wasn't expecting her to agree so easily.

"It's a surprise," I tell her.

"I don't do surprises."

"Well, the only thing I pinky promised not to discuss was how the way you kissed me has me all kinds of fucked up. I promised not to talk about how I'm unsure whether you paint or kiss better."

"Maverick!" she shrieks, slapping me right on the bicep.

"What? We aren't talking about it." I smirk at her, dramatically rubbing the spot she just hit.

Veronica narrows her eyes at me before walking past me and

climbing the steps. "You're exhausting," she says at the same time she pushes the door open at the top of the stairs.

I race up after her, stepping out into the hallway and then following her into the kitchen.

I keep a careful gaze on her as she rifles around in the refrigerator, clearly looking for something.

"Oh my god, I might kill him," she mutters, half her body inside the refrigerator.

"Aspen?" I ask, propping my elbows up against the counter next to the fridge.

"I was looking forward to eating that protein bar and it's gone." She slams the door shut, letting out a large sigh with the motion.

"Don't worry about it. We'll get food on our way."

"Are you going to tell me *where* we'll be on our way to?"

"Nope," I say, standing up from the counter to my full height.

We're standing close to each other, closer than I anticipated. I'm caught in the moment, staring at the indentation above her top lip. When I look up from her lips, I find her eyes on me— watching intently. I can hear her soft intake of breath. My ears don't miss how she exhales it slowly.

My hand reaches out on its own accord. I don't know where I want to touch first, my eyes taking in all of my options. I reach a finger out and trace over her shoulder blade, deftly moving her hair so it falls down her back. I slowly trace the slope of her shoulder blade then dip down. The skin of her collarbone is warm underneath my fingertip as I commit the hollow above her collarbone to muscle memory.

My index finger follows a small line of freckles all the way down to the ink permanently etched on her skin. I have the urge to trace the slopes and planes of the cursive font with my mouth, dipping and curving with every stroke. I don't give into the urge, but I do follow every stroke of the handwriting with the tip of my finger.

Veronica's hand flies up and tightly wraps around my forearm, her long nails biting into my skin.

Is it fucked up of me to want her nails to leave a mark on my skin? A reminder that some part of her is feeling a fraction of what I'm feeling?

Her blue eyes face off in a silent conversation with my own. Neither one of us uses words, but somehow, we manage to say everything.

I know I promised not to talk about what's happening between the two of us, but I'm slowly starting to come to terms with the fact that *something* about Veronica is making me fall back on every single promise I've ever made.

27

VERONICA

"Okay, I've really tried to not say anything, but where the hell are you taking me?" I look over at Maverick in the driver's seat, trying for the hundredth time to get him to spill on where we're going.

He's as tight lipped as ever, though, because all he does is give me that panty-dropping smirk. His fingers flex around the steering wheel, his lips silently moving along to the song on the radio.

We've been in Maverick's SUV for thirty minutes now and I have no idea where we are. We left the suburban town of our campus and went straight to BFE. No matter what direction I look in, all the eye can see is fields of wheat. Maybe a few cows. A house every so often. But mostly, it's fields.

I guess that's what I get for choosing a state in the middle of the country to go to college. I just didn't want to be anywhere near an ocean.

I'm about to complain more when I get an answer—in the form of a flip of his turn signal and a turn onto a dirt path. My back straightens in the leather seat as I try to get a better look out the window.

I pull on the bottom of my dress. Even though fall is in full swing in Kansas, it's a warm day. My stomach growls beneath the fabric, reminding me I still haven't eaten today. The smell of the pizza in the backseat only makes it worse. Maverick didn't tell me where we were taking the pizza that he picked up on our way out of civilization, but he did ask what my favorite kind was.

"Just one more minute," he says, adjusting his hips on the seat. Both of us jostle around as he drives down the unpaved road.

"For the record, I'm never agreeing to go somewhere with you ever again." The last part comes out with a grunt because we hit a bump so large it causes my thighs to slap against each other in the seat.

Maverick chuckles, looking at me out of the corner of his eye. "Welcome to the Midwest, V."

"You suck at surprises," I mumble, reaching up to grab the *oh shit* handle. I'm two seconds away from telling Maverick to turn the car around while simultaneously feasting on a slice of pizza right here in the front seat. My mouth opens to say just that when we break through the tree line and end up in the middle of a field.

A field that surrounds a small lake.

Or is that a pond?

I don't know what the hell to call it besides a small body of water seated right in the middle of a vast expanse of orange and yellows.

I look in every direction to take it all in. Maverick drives down the barely-there path before parking near the edge of the water. I'm too busy looking at my surroundings to hear what he says once the car stops.

I didn't expect something so beautiful.

The water sits still in front of us, not a single crease marring the smooth surface.

Maverick puts his hand on my knee. "Veronica?"

"Huh?" I ask, looking away from the blowing wheat in the wind to look at him.

That dimple of his makes an appearance on his cheek. "What do you think?"

I look at his smile then back out to the land. "Oh, it's okay."

He takes his hand off my thigh. "Ready to go out there?"

He reaches over me to pop open my door handle, his arm barely grazing over my chest.

As soon as my door is open, I'm hit with a smell very different from the ocean air I'm used to. This is clean, fresh, the scent of the wheat adding some musk to it.

The sound of Maverick's door slamming causes me to jump. I look over my shoulder to find him opening the door to the backseat to grab the pizza.

I tentatively step one leg out of the car, making sure there's solid footing underneath my foot before I completely get out. The dried grass crunches underneath my boots as I walk to the front of the SUV. A few yards away from us sits the calm body of water.

There's a large forest to our right filled with various degrees of dying leaves, with some scattered about on the field. Some still cling to their old branches. I've always found it interesting that we find leaves most beautiful in the stages just before they die.

Maverick whistles, causing me to jump. When I look at him, I notice his hands are full.

He's clutching a bag in his left hand, and something clinks around in it when he goes to shift the blanket that's propped over his shoulder. He has the pizza box in his other hand. "Follow me." He nods his head toward the water and I fall in step behind him.

"This land is actually owned by my grandfather," Maverick says as he tries to kick a path for us through the tall grass. "It's been in our family for generations. I spent so much of my life running through these fields with Lil."

He stops directly in front of me, a few steps away from the peaceful water. I almost crash into him because I'm admiring the land, imagining him and Lily running around here as children.

Maverick juggles everything but the blanket in one hand as he uses the other hand to fluff out the blanket. I end up helping him before he almost drops the pizza box in the process. He's brought us to a flat part of grass, the field a little shorter here by the water than where we parked. I help him lay the blanket flat, listening to him rattle on about how he grew up here. He mentions something about how many ticks he's pulled off himself after playing in this field and I smile.

Once the blanket is flat, Maverick places his items on top of it before sitting down. He raises his eyebrows and smirks, waiting for me to follow his lead. I hesitantly look around the space, making sure there aren't any visible ticks or creatures near me.

I sit on the edge of the blanket across from him, stretching my legs out in front of me and pulling the dress down my thighs at the same time. I cross my combat boots over my ankles, the pink toes of the boots resting right by Maverick's knees.

"What do you think?" he asks as he props the pizza box open, the smell of the cheese and pepperoni making my mouth salivate. "Shit. I forgot plates." Maverick looks at me, a grimace on his face. He cautiously watches me, like he's checking if it's a big deal.

I shrug and reach across the blanket to grab a pepperoni slice. My eyes stay trained on his as I take a large bite of it, not caring about a plate at all. I want to moan over the pizza it's so *good*. My jaw slowly chews, savoring the flavor of what's probably the best pizza I've ever had.

Maverick mimics my motion, reaching in and plucking a slice for himself. He takes a large bite, staring at me as he chews. His large Adam's apple moves as he swallows. "Another one of your contradictions, Veronica," he says before taking another bite of his pizza. "You better watch out, before you know it, I'll have them all figured out."

I take another bite to avoid responding to him right away. Him figuring me out is exactly what I'm afraid of. I'm terrified that he'll figure everything out about me, and still want to stay.

I would rather him run. He's too good not to run.

Connor knew all about my shattered pieces, and he chose to stay. Look what it did to him.

"What do you mean, my *contradictions*?" I use the corner of the blanket to wipe the grease off my hands once I finish my pizza.

Maverick stares at the last bite of his slice before he begins to talk. "I don't know, it's something I kind of noticed about you on the first day I met you. You're just kind of a contradiction. You have this attitude that's supposed to scare everyone away and seems—"

"Dark?" I ask with a smirk.

He tips his pizza slice at me. "Yeah, dark. And it sounds dumb now that I'm saying it out loud, but you just have this air about you that doesn't strike me as girly. Yet you walk around in the girliest, sweetest pair of pink floral boots. You scream goth and spoiled rich girl all at the same time."

"What's wrong with being both?" I ask.

Maverick grins, his mouth still full of pizza.

I wait for him to finish chewing, bumping his knee with one of my boots that, apparently, he's put a lot of thought into.

"You can be both," he says. "I actually *love* that you're both, but that doesn't make you any less of a contradiction." He points to the pizza box, silently inquiring if I want more.

I shake my head at him, my appetite curbed for the time being. "Tell me more about these *contradictions* I have." My hands pull at the strands of my hair as I look over at him.

His back is facing the water as he pulls his legs out of a cross-legged position and stretches them out across the blanket. We both sit with our feet outstretched on the blanket. Maverick's propped elbow now rests right next to my foot.

"On the day I first met you, I remember thinking how odd it was that a face as beautiful and serene as yours could be giving a look of hate like the one you had on, staring at that damn board," he says.

My teeth pull on my lip as I think back to that day, back to that dumb quote and how angry it made me. "I see." I pull my eyes off the water to look at Maverick again.

He's watching me closely, his fingers playing with a blade of grass. He doesn't say anything; he just stares at me for a few moments longer with a thoughtful look on his face. Then, his gaze travels to the expanse of land around us.

It really is beautiful to look at. It's about midafternoon, and the field is mostly silent around us. Every now and then, you can hear the rustling of the field when the wind blows. It's peaceful, the way the tall grass dances back and forth with the breeze. We stay silent for a while, the both of us lost in our own worlds.

Maverick is too busy picking at the grass to notice me staring at him. I seize the opportunity to analyze him without having him analyze me in return. He wears a pair of jeans, and the same Adidas on his feet from the day we met.

The hoodie he has on is simple and black. My eyes make it to his face—the face I hadn't ever wanted to admit was *so* strikingly handsome. That straight nose of his is sitting above his perfect set of lips. A set of lips I'm still reeling from after feeling them against my own. The way they moved against mine is something I will never be able to wash from my memory—no matter how hard I try.

I follow the sharp edge of his cheekbone, to the exact spot I've seen tension and frustration apparent on him. I keep moving up his jawline until I reach his hair, the hair that's dark brown and perfectly long at the top. I wonder how long I would have denied how badly my fingers had always itched to run through the locks, to grab onto them and force his head against mine.

And those eyes. Those blue eyes the same color of the ocean that took my first love from me. The eyes that just looked up at me, framed in long dark eyelashes.

We maintain eye contact for one, two, three seconds before I ruin the moment and finally ask, "What happened with Selma?"

28

VERONICA

I AWAIT HIS RESPONSE, my heart on edge. I know he wouldn't be here with me unless he was fully single, even if I had no intentions of taking things any further with us.

But I also know we're past an innocent friendship at this point.

What I don't know is what could have happened between the two of them to cause them to break up after so many years —or why he's chosen to be here with *me*.

So many questions run through my head while I wait for him to answer. I almost wish it wasn't so silent in this field—it leaves me too alone with my thoughts. An agonizing amount of time passes before he finally responds.

"We broke up. It was a long time coming, actually. Neither of us realized that. Or at least, neither of us wanted to admit it." Maverick sits up and pulls his legs toward him, his knees resting right in front of his chest. His body now sits closer to mine.

I could reach out and touch his face if I wanted to. "Admit what, exactly?" I trace the pattern of the blanket with my finger, giving myself something to do while he continues to explain. I'm still staring down at the lines on the blanket when he speaks again.

"Selma will always be one of the most important people in

my life. That will never change. But Selma and I haven't been *in* love with each other for a long time, if ever. I love her with every single part of me, but that isn't the same as being *in love* with her. And she finally realized that. So, she left. She ended it." The emotion is clear in his voice.

Whatever happened between them, I can tell it was hard for him, something he's still processing.

"Are you okay that things ended with her?" I'm nervous to hear his answer. I want him to say yes. I want him to be fully okay that he isn't with her anymore. Which is completely selfish of me, because I don't want to just be her replacement. Though I'm not naïve enough to try and convince myself I won't be hurt if he says he isn't okay about it.

Who is this guy and how have I let him in like this?

How could I allow myself to get hurt by another man?

More importantly, how could I allow myself to possibly hurt another person again?

"Look at me," he says, snapping me out of my thoughts.

I didn't realize I was still avoiding looking at him until now. I raise my head, doing as he says. Our faces are too close. But I don't dare move away. I'm struck by the look of determination on his face.

He reaches for my hand on the blanket, his pinky wrapping around mine. I stare at our intertwined fingers for a few moments, looking at the contrast of his tan pinky against my pale one. My gaze leaves our hands and I look back up at him.

His stare is intense as he says, "I'm glad things ended with her. They needed to end. I don't want back with her. I don't know what exactly I want."

His eyes drop to the words written underneath my collarbone for a brief moment.

"But I do know the relationship Selma and I had wasn't healthy," he says. "I think I was trying to make her into someone she wasn't, so I could feel better about myself. And I think she was too afraid of being who she really was. It wasn't a good combination. We were stuck in the roles we let each other play."

"But you were together so long." I move my hand so not

only my pinky touches his, but the rest of my fingers brush against his as well.

He lets out a breath, long and steady like the breeze blowing the grass around us. "Yeah, well, I'm starting to learn that time isn't everything. I was with her for a long time and never felt the things I've felt recently."

"Maverick," I begin, after he fully wraps his hand around mine. I look down.

We're holding hands.

He pulls my hand so it rests on the top of his knees. His head leans down and gives my knuckles a featherlight kiss. It makes everything in my body tighten. I feel like a rubber band that's been pulled and pulled, and I'm on the brink of snapping.

His touch might make me snap.

Or maybe those lips.

Or the look on his face that's so vulnerable, so trusting, so determined that it sends my heart into overdrive. I have feelings for him, feelings I don't understand at all, but they're there—hiding underneath my insecurities and facades, ready to make an appearance.

"I told you I can't do this with you." My voice comes out hoarse, the scratchy tone filling the silence around us. My fingers grip his tightly as I look at him, conveying how serious I am.

"We don't have to talk about it. Really," he says. "I'm going to be selfish and take you in whatever way I can get you. Even if it's just as friends. But I need you to know that I feel something for you I haven't felt before. It's new for me, and I'm still trying to understand it but…I have to make sure you know that I'm looking at you. I'm looking at every bruised part of you and I'm not afraid by any of it."

I want to cry—and by the way my throat starts to close up, I know that I'm close. I don't want to cry in front of him. I don't want him to know how much his words mean to me. I try to think of a way to respond, but my resolve to push him away is slowly breaking.

There's only so much good I can do.

There's only so many times I can try to avoid being selfish before I break.

It's in my nature.

I'm about to give into him. To admit that my heart might actually feel something for him, too. But I don't get the chance because he makes the first move. His hands reach for the narrow of my waist and pull. In one fluid moment, he's turned me around and pulled my back to his chest. I sit nestled in between his long legs, staring out at the view. I'm completely enveloped by him. His arms wrap around my middle, gently enough that if I want to move away from him, I can.

I should get away, but this feels too nice. It feels good to lean against him. To feel the way his strong abdominal muscles flex against my back. To feel the warmth of his toned arms around me. I love the way his head rests on my shoulder—right next to my own.

"Will you tell me about your last relationship now?" he asks softly.

His question stuns me and makes me want to weep at the same time. Here is this man, in the midst of his own mess, and somehow, he still cares about mine.

I don't know how I found him. How fate had this hilarious way of punishing me by putting someone so perfectly imperfect in front of me and expecting me to stay away.

But I'm about to raise my white flag—to stop pushing him away and have him for myself.

29

MAVERICK

WE STAND in front of her bedroom door, the both of us utterly silent after our trip to my grandfather's property.

I want her to invite me inside.

I need her to ask me to stay with her tonight.

For her to admit that she feels something for me, too.

I wait for her to tell me that the hours by the lake discussing Connor and so many other things meant something to her. I just need *some* kind of reassurance that this isn't all in my head. But more than that, I need reassurance that she'll allow whatever's developing between us to happen—or attempt to happen. Judging by the way she acted today, it seemed like she might be doing just that.

Veronica had allowed me to hold her as we sat in the field.

We watched the sun set behind the lake with our bodies intertwined.

We didn't kiss, but our bodies said more to each other than our lips ever could.

In the soft brush of our hands. When she absentmindedly traced the muscles of my forearms. When she let out the quietest gasp when my fingers rested on the bare skin of her leg. So many touches that felt like...something *more*.

"Thank you for coming with me today," I finally say, breaking the awkward silence between us.

She looks up at me, giving me a smile—and for some reason, it seems sad. "You kind of kidnapped me."

"You kind of let me."

Her lips pull up even more. "True." She folds her arms over her chest, leaning back to rest against the wall next to her door.

Aspen's footsteps echo above us as he moves around his room. We both look to the ceiling before looking back at each other.

"Tonight…" I start, rubbing my hands against my pants. "Tonight, can you just allow yourself to look at me the way you want to? Can we just explore this thing that's happening between us, for at least tonight?" My hand gestures between the two of us before I continue on, too chickenshit to look at her. "We don't need to decide if we want to date, or put any label on it. But for the last few hours, all I could think about was your body against mine. And by the way you reacted to my touch, I think you were thinking the same thing."

I step closer to her, pleading with her with my eyes for her to agree. "Just one night. Can we allow ourselves one night?"

I'm desperate. My heart beats so fast in my chest as I wait for her answer.

And then it plummets.

Because I know the look in her eyes as she looks back up at me, and it's not one that holds the answer I want. The walls she had slowly started to let down raise back up in an instant.

"Maverick, you need to go back to Selma," she states.

What the actual fuck?

The look on my face must give me away because she continues to try and fill in the blanks. I feel the muscle in my jaw tighten. My jaw clenches, trying not to spew everything going through my head right now.

She lifts her chin in a defiant way, so defiant I can almost hear her walls click back into place. The same unreachable height around her heart they were when we first met.

"I'm not the girl you want," Veronica says. "Selma was good for you. You want me because I'm a challenge. It'll wear off, I promise. Go back to her. You were meant for each other."

I laugh—a bitter, self-deprecating laugh—because *oh my god*, she hasn't listened to anything I've said.

My feet step back from her, my hands going to the top of my head and resting there. I make sure to take a deep breath before I respond. A million things go through my head. I want to lash out at her. I want to yell, scream, do something dramatic to let her know that no matter what happens between her and I that Selma and I won't be getting back together—ever.

Three, two, one...

"Okay, first of all, this has nothing to do with my breakup with Selma. I told you, we aren't—and weren't—meant to be together. Simple as that. So, please don't try and push me away because you think you're the thing that's standing between me and her. You're a lot of things to me, Veronica, but the one thing you aren't is the reason Selma and I won't get back together."

My chest heaves as I try to pull air into my lungs. "And second of all, yes, I want you. I probably want you more than I have ever wanted anything. But I'm not standing here asking for anything more than a night. Because I'm not used to this feeling. I don't understand it and I'm just trying to work through it by allowing us to figure it out—together."

"I can't," she mutters. With those two words, a tear runs down her cheek.

I want to wipe it away, to give her a hug or do something to console her. But I'm not perfect, and I can only take rejection so many times before giving up. My feet stay planted in their spot on the basement floor. I can still hear Aspen walking around upstairs, but I don't let my eyes wander to the ceiling again. I'm solely focused on her, trying to read everything her body is telling me—the things her mouth refuses to speak.

"You can't, or you won't?" The words are quiet when they come out of my mouth, but they apparently still hit home by the way her head viciously starts to shake.

"Does it matter?" The blue in her eyes is crystal-clear when she looks at me.

I pull in air through my nose, my fingers threading through the top of my hair. I take a few steps away from her.

Space.

I need space.

I didn't realize she had the power to break me yet, but here I stand with a gut-wrenching feeling in my chest and a sinking feeling in my stomach that feels a lot like breaking.

"No, Veronica. I guess it doesn't." I stare her down, giving her the opportunity to say something else—to argue, to change her mind—but she doesn't.

She just stares at me, her cheeks wet with tears, not relenting.

I nod, coming to understand that maybe she'll always be a *what if* for me. I slowly start to retreat to the basement stairs. I finally look away from her, unable to see her pain for another second.

This is where I normally give up whatever *I* want, just to make sure the other person is happy.

But here? I can't do it.

I can't be the white knight in this scenario—her *savior*. There's too much at stake for me to risk in order to save her. My heart, namely.

So, I walk away from her.

I walk away even though it breaks me a little more to hear the quiet sob breaking from her throat as my feet hit the first stair.

I'm halfway up them when her voice fills the basement.

"I've already given my heart away once," she says. "After pulling Connor's lifeless body out of the water, I vowed I would never do it again."

It's quiet, so quiet I almost don't hear it, but I do hear the emotion in her voice that sneaks through. The way it scratches with her words, the way the words drag out—painfully.

My forehead hits the basement door as I reach the top, trying to pull myself together enough to actually walk away.

My hand is on the doorknob when I respond to her. "I didn't demand your heart. I just asked for a night."

With that, I barrel through the door and rush to my room, where I slam my door behind me.

30

MAVERICK

FOUR DAYS.

Four days since Veronica and I have uttered a word to each other.

She barely even looks at me when we share the same space, which isn't often because she's been doing her best to completely avoid me.

However, it's not all on her. I don't want to say anything to her either.

I've said everything I wanted to say.

She didn't want it, she didn't want to try. I'm exhausted by her.

When she avoids me, I make sure to avoid her back. If I hear those boots coming up the stairs, I retreat to my bedroom. It feels childish, but it's how I'm coping with the rejection, with the lack of even wanting to try.

Poor Aspen is stuck in the middle of our drama. He shifts between spending time with me in the living room and spending time with Veronica in the basement. His constant pestering about what happened has almost driven me to insanity. I understand he just wants to know how and why things changed between Veronica and I so quickly, but I don't have it in me to try to explain.

Now, I sit on my bed, gazing at the self-portrait Veronica

painted of herself. My finger runs over the oil paint. It dried long ago, but it still has a bumpy texture that makes her brush-strokes obvious.

I stare at the girl in the painting. I want to know how Veronica felt when she painted this piece. If it helped her, or if it just reminded her of everything she hates about herself.

I wish she could see the image through my eyes. The way the curves of her inward shoulders don't show defeat, but a battle that she refused to lose. How the blurred and smeared edges don't mean her life is out of focus, but instead, coming into it—day by day.

I wish she could see all of her and her past through my eyes. Because when I look at her, I don't see someone worthy of feeling guilt, I see someone who survived hell.

I find myself once again thinking back to the day I first met her, the way she looked so dejected and hateful while staring at that innocent self-help quote.

Her pain was so clear from the beginning—if only I'd paid closer attention to the warnings.

I can't blame her for where things stand between us now. She never made any false promises to me. She wasn't cold because she was playing hard to get; she was cold because she didn't want to be caught.

But I've been wearing rose-colored glasses when it comes to her.

It's hilarious, because I truly thought I could have been the one to change her mind about love. About relationships. What a naïve asshole I was.

Of course I couldn't change her.

No one could change her but herself.

And she doesn't *want* to change.

It's still a sad realization, because the only thing that needs to change about her is her own opinion of herself. Everything else about her is flawed but beautiful—just like those imperfections she likes to paint so much.

I wish she'd realize that Connor's death wasn't her fault. That she'd stop viewing herself as the villain and realize she's just another human being who's been dealt a shitty hand in life.

As I stare at the girl in the painting, I wonder what could have happened with us if she hadn't completely shut down after the death of her first love. If, instead of closing everyone out like she said she had, she'd allowed herself to grieve.

What would she have been like if someone had looked her in the eye and told her it was just an accident?

Would she have held onto the guilt no matter what anyone said?

Or would she have been able to forgive herself, maybe even tolerate herself after some time?

My finger's still tracing over the curves of her brushstrokes when I realize it doesn't matter.

It's something she needs to realize on her own. And for her sake, I hope she finds that peace within herself one day.

Just as my mind continues to wander while I look down at her self-created image, encompassed by oil paints, the artist herself flings my bedroom door wide open.

31

VERONICA

"WHAT THE FUCK, MAVERICK!" I plow through his door, not paying any attention to the fact that he may have had it shut for a reason. I push it open to find a shirtless Maverick sitting on his bed.

He tosses something to the ground as I barge through the door. His body flies off the bed so fast he's basically a blur of motion—a blur with a pretty damn good six-pack. I haven't laid eyes on those muscles on him for a bit now.

But I shove that out of my mind as I inch my way closer to him, not even worrying about hiding my fury. "You bought my paintings?" I'm so angry that I see red. When I took my pieces to Clementine's gallery, I didn't expect anyone I *know* to buy one of them—let alone all of them.

He wasn't supposed to intervene. They were *my* imperfections. *Mine.*

Even though some of them weren't my own, *I* painted them. Labored over them.

Hell, I even cried over them.

He wasn't supposed to freaking buy them.

His hands go up defensively. "You took them to a gallery to sell."

I sigh, the air leaving my body in a blast that both of us can hear. "To sell to a *stranger*. Not to you, Maverick! It can't be you." My hands are on my hips, adrenaline pumping through my body. I haven't been this pissed in a long time. It seems like a betrayal that he bought those paintings without telling me, though I can't tell why.

"Well, I now own them, Veronica. So, you can be pissed at me, but that won't change the fact that they're mine."

I want to slap him.

God, do I want to fucking slap him.

My fingers itch to strike that perfectly chiseled cheek of his. "I'm so mad at you right now! They weren't yours to buy! How *dare* you come in and buy something so personal to me?!" My foot stomps and I know I look like a fucking *child*—but I don't care. I don't know what else to do with all the rage filling my body right now.

"What would you have preferred, Veronica? That some random person hang them up in their house as a fucking *talking piece* at some boring dinner they're hosting with their asshole country club friends? The price tags were high. I wasn't about to let some pretentious asshole who didn't know anything about you hang those up on their wall as a fucking accent piece."

My eyes focus on the vein pulsing at his neck—an indicator that his anger is also escalating.

"It wasn't your decision to make!" I seethe, taking a step closer to him. A step that puts me so close to him I could reach out and run my hand over his abdominal muscles if I dared.

But right now, the only touch I crave to give him is a slap on that infuriatingly perfect sculpted cheek.

I feel violated. Violated that he took it upon himself to buy things so personal to me.

It doesn't matter that some of the paintings were of him; it matters that he knew how personal they were to me.

He must have been able to tell the morning I put them in my trunk that I never wanted to see them again.

It's violating, because part of me woke up when Clementine told me who bought them.

If I'm being honest with myself, I'm not pissed that he bought them. I'm pissed at how my heart did an odd, disgusting flutter in my chest when I found out the buyer—of *all* of them

—was him. I'm well aware of the price tags that were on each of them. And now that I know he has them in his possession, it makes me feel completely unhinged.

"Half of them were my god damn face. What do you mean it wasn't my *place?*" he yells back.

I can tell he's pissed now. His dark eyebrows are drawn together on his face, those long fingers of his tap against his thigh so quick they're almost a blur.

"I never wanted to see them again!" I take a step closer to him, one that would have put me chest-to-chest to him if he hadn't just taken a step back.

"Then don't see them again." His voice is condescending. As if it's such an obvious answer. He keeps taking steps backward until his back makes a soft *thump* against the wall.

"I can't just *pretend* you don't have them, Maverick. They are mine. Mine—and *only mine!* They aren't something that you come in and buy because you're trying to save me from myself or help me with money or whatever the hell your motives were behind it." I put my hands on my hips, focusing on taking deep breaths in and out because the thumping in my chest is too erratic right now. I scan around his bedroom—a room I've never been in until now.

It's surprisingly clean. Boring, but clean.

"I'm not trying to save you, Veronica!" His hands fly up and he yanks at his hair in frustration. His chest dives in and out, over and over again. "Jesus Christ, if you could get out of your own head for two seconds, you would realize I didn't do this for you. I did it for me. *Me.*" His knuckles pound against his bare chest. "I was being fucking selfish because the thought of some asshole hanging those up on their wall drove me insane. After I saw the emotion on your face after you spent all night painting them, I couldn't see them end up somewhere random. Something about the way you looked at me when you allowed me to see your work broke me in half, okay? I didn't buy them for you. I bought them for me. Because I wanted to look at them and remember the moment I saw a piece of you that you kept hidden from the rest of the world. Are you happy now?" His shoulders sag in defeat.

I don't breathe a word at first. My head spins with his confession. I want him to look at me right now, so I can read the emotion in the depths of his eyes.

But he stares at something across the room. His eyes look in any direction but mine. He hasn't looked at me for days now. I'm not the only one that's been playing the cold shoulder game.

My mind races for a few moments longer before I make a mistake. A mistake I'm willing to face the consequences for because there's nothing else I can think of at the moment.

"You don't even know the definition of selfish." And with that I close the distance between us. I push him against the wall and kiss him, attacking him with my mouth. I'm still so angry, but I take it out on his lips.

I expect him not to kiss me back, to push me away and say something to make me feel guilty for wanting him like this.

But he doesn't do that.

As soon as my lips assault his, he's ready, as if he's been waiting for this longer than I have.

We attack each other in a frenzy I can't explain. Our chests collide together. My teeth bang against his. Neither one of us can decide where we want our hands to land. I thread my fingers through that dark hair at the top of his head and yank him closer to me, pulling him down so he arches over me. I rub my body against his as our lips move together in a crashing symphony.

His hands wrap around my waist, fisting the fabric of my sweater in his fingers. "Holy fuck," he says, his lips running down my throat in a slow descent that fires off so many nerve endings in my abdomen. His teeth clamp down on the skin of my shoulder, causing me to moan desperately, my hips arching against his.

I grab the strong line of his jaw and guide his lips back to mine, already missing how they fell against mine in perfect rhythm. When given the opportunity, I take his full bottom lip— where his scar sits—and bite down. I pull it out as he lets out a moan himself. My teeth let go, but I go back for more and kiss the spot where my teeth just were. My tongue caresses the jagged line, committing it to memory. If I thought I could paint it before, it doesn't compare to how I could now. Now that I've had the chance to become *very* acquainted with it.

The strong hands on my waist slide underneath my sweater. They tighten against my skin before Maverick lifts me up, spinning us, then pushes me against the wall. I'm now face-to-face with him without having to pull his neck down. My legs twist around his hips, gripping him so hard there's no way he could get rid of me at this point.

His deep eyes stare at me for one long, agonizing moment. I wish I could be in his head right now, but the thought leaves as soon as his lips are back on mine. He kneads at my ass and I suddenly wish I didn't have leggings on. I want to feel his skin against mine. If I didn't have them on right now, I'd be able to feel the flex of his muscles against my inner thighs.

It's something I desperately need.

"You taste better than I could have ever fantasized," he murmurs.

My thighs clench around him.

32

MAVERICK

"Have you been thinking about me, Maverick?" she whispers. Her legs are wrapped so tightly around me that it hurts to breathe, the soft skin of her thighs rubbing against my hip bones.

"Even though every part of me didn't want to," I respond, pulling her hair so her throat is exposed. My mouth licks and nips at her creamy white skin. As difficult as she is in person, I thought it would be hard to get a reaction out of her, but it's the opposite. She sighs and moans with every press of my body against hers.

Her hands fly up to my chest, pushing against it—hard. "Oh my god, Selma." Her eyes are wide—regret etched in every single line on her face.

I miss the feel of her legs around me as soon she unravels them. I help her catch her balance as her bare feet thud against the carpeted floor. I don't move my hands from the small of her waist.

I force her face to look at me by grasping her chin lightly. "Selma and I aren't a couple anymore. You know that."

Her perfect mouth opens widely. Her jaw works open and then closes as she tries to figure out what to say.

And I understand why—because it feels odd for me to even *say*, a part of me still not used to the words.

Ever since Selma and I broke up, I told myself I wouldn't allow myself to put my hands on Veronica for months—if given the chance. I didn't want to come off as that douchebag who bounced from one chick to another. But that was obviously another lie I told to myself to feel like I was doing the right thing.

Now I know that doing the right thing can go to hell if it means I get to taste Veronica again.

It's all I've thought about since the night we played spin the bottle.

Selma and I are over. I was faithful to her, always. That has to count for something. And I know I should give it time before I try whatever *this* is with Veronica, but I'm not strong enough to follow my own advice.

I knew the moment *before* my lips first pressed against hers, during that game of spin the bottle, that I would never be able to forget it. And I did it anyway.

Now, I can admit I need her lips on me just as badly as I want to unravel the tangle of lies she tells herself every night to cope with her trauma. Desperately. Passionately. Without any thought of the consequences.

"So, I'm the god damn rebound?" She crosses her arm over her chest, glaring at me like I'm the first person on her shit list.

The pout on her face is adorable.

I want to wipe it off with my lips.

"You're not the rebound. You're just—I just don't know, Veronica. You're just *you*. I've been thinking of you for longer than I should've been and now that we've started this, I'm not sure I can stop. At least not tonight." I reach between us and play with a long strand of her hair. I twist it around my finger, giving her some time to think it through.

If I feel her lips again, it'll be because she's finally admitting that *something* has ignited between us and she feels the need to let it burn wild as well.

I try not to think about what will happen if she denies me again. I might crumble. I'm not above getting on my knees and begging her to give us a chance. Even if that chance is only for a single night.

Veronica doesn't make me wait long. Her tiny hands press against my chest until I'm forced to walk backward. The backs of my thighs hit my bed frame as we fall together onto my black sheets.

"I'm not a rebound," she states, climbing over me until she's on top of me.

"You're not a rebound," I repeat.

"This can't be more than sex. You know that, right?" Her hand slides down my abs. She takes her time, occasionally stopping to trace the outline of muscles. Those slim fingers slip into the waistband of my joggers and I am done for.

"Veronica?" I purposefully ignore her last comment. Not willing to admit this isn't *just sex* for me.

Her big eyes look at me. They're wide with mischief as she starts to stroke me up and down. Those perfectly arched eyebrows raise in question.

"Stop overthinking this. Let me kiss you until you forget about your rules. I don't want you thinking about anything other than where my mouth will land on you next." At my words, her hand stills on me and I use it to my advantage. I flip us over so that I now lie over her.

Blonde strands of hair fan out around her. I love the way the blonde looks against my black sheets. My arms are on either side of her head. It feels like we're in our own world. My body hovers over hers and I stare into her eyes for a long moment. I wish I could crawl inside that pretty head of hers and live in there—get acquainted with what she tells herself.

But since I can't, I'll settle for getting to know every agonizingly beautiful part of her body.

Bracing myself on my elbow, I use my free hand to trace over her silhouette, starting at her heart-shaped face. Continuing down her long neck, I feel her pulse underneath my fingertip, beating in a fast rhythm that rivals my own. I absentmindedly trace over the tattoo written on her collar bone.

My mind skips back to the moment I first noticed it. It was the first night I saw her skin and felt something. I didn't understand it then, but I do now.

My hand continues its descent until I trace over the peak of her breasts. Her quick intake of air when I circle around her nipple sends the rest of my blood to my dick. I reach the bottom of her sweater, looking at her for permission to take it off.

"Get it the fuck off," she says breathlessly, making me chuckle. That attitude of hers is something else.

We both lift up to remove it. She manages to tear it off in one swift movement and I'm rewarded with the sight of a great expanse of creamy white skin.

My eyes roam over the skin I used to refuse to admire. Now, I can't find where I want to look most. She's wearing a bra that looks more like a sports bra than a normal bra. But it's made of lace that I can see right through. Feeling the need to get even more acquainted with her body, I lean down and suck on the fabric right over her nipple.

Veronica yelps underneath me, her hands clawing at my back. I take the time to get to know both breasts before I slide my mouth down her soft stomach. The slope of her ribcage rises and falls as I make a slow descent.

"Jesus Christ," Veronica mutters when I start to play with the waistband of her leggings. She has her head tilted back and her hips arched up, waiting for me.

My finger dips into her pants, and I fall in love with the sounds she makes as I explore her.

"Off. I need them off." Her hips raise until I take the hint, peeling the leggings off to expose all of her to me.

I find she has nothing on underneath the leggings.

I see all of her—something I desperately need.

I bite down on her jutting hip bones, licking the spot where my teeth just were.

"Lower, Maverick. Go lower." Her hands tangle in my hair as she pushes my head down, raising her hips so I reach her center quicker.

I give her what she wants.

I go lower.

33

VERONICA

We fit together perfectly.

Once he was inside me, it felt like a small part of me found myself.

I found myself in how his mouth worshipped my lips.

In how his fingers tangled in my hair.

A little bit more of me *made sense* as he chanted my name all night. The soft whispers of it. The loud groans. The way my name came out of his mouth like gravel as we each chased our release—together.

I found myself in the lazy strokes of his fingers on my skin.

In the empty conversation as we lay in his bed, our limbs tangled together.

I found myself.

I found myself and it terrified me.

Because as a part of me started to make sense, another part of me wanted to rebel. That part of me couldn't forget what I had been through, what I made a vow to myself about.

And I still stand true to my oath. To never love another man; to never let another man love me.

So, now I have to live with this consequence of giving in to him.

Because I gave him a part of me, with no intentions of taking a part of him.

It felt empty, wrong.

But I found myself. I found myself in him and it scared me.

It left me with less of myself, and none of him. I wasn't *willing* to take anything from him.

And it felt empty, *so wrong*.

34

VERONICA

THE NEXT COUPLE of weeks pass by in a blur. I work, I go to school, and I lose myself in Maverick.

The first time we slept together, I was determined not to let it happen again—but he's an addiction I don't want to kick.

Any spare moment we have, we find ourselves tangled up in bed.

Except for now, when we find ourselves actually *out* of the house for once.

We've joined Lily, Aspen, Tristan and some other friends at Lenny's. I wouldn't admit it to anyone out loud, but I truly *enjoy* hanging out with them.

I would rather be at home with Maverick's face between my thighs, but...

Lily and I sit across from each other in the large booth our party takes up. The boys are playing pool, leaving us alone here. We've spent the last twenty minutes discussing our workout routines.

But now, she becomes serious as she faces me. "What's going on with you and my brother?" Lily takes a long drink out of her beer as I almost spit mine out all over the table. She raises her dark eyebrows at me and reaches across the table to hand me a napkin, the napkin wiggling in the air. "Might want to clean yourself up."

I glare at her, taking the napkin from her and wiping around my mouth. When I look down, I find that a small amount of my beer has landed on my sheer bodysuit. "What's going on with you and Aspen?" I counter. It comes out bitchy, but if she wants to get personal, two can play that game.

I've noticed the way her eyes have lingered on Aspen tonight, longer than they should. Their normal banter has been kicked up to ten. If I were a betting girl, I'd say there's been a new development between the two of them. I was going to mind my own business for once, but since she decided to bring up my situation with Maverick, all bets are off.

She rolls her eyes, downing the rest of her beer, then slaps it down on the table. "Aspen and I had sex."

My eyebrows shoot up, and I lean across the table, anxious to hear more.

"And let's just say…it was my first time getting, you know, busy with somebody else. It freaked him out. We yelled at each other. Now I hate him." Her eyes focus on where he's playing a game of pool with Maverick.

Aspen seems to be telling some kind of story, because he animatedly spins his hands around as Maverick nods his head every now and then.

Maverick must sense my gaze, because he looks my way and winks—fucking *winks*—and it does something to my stomach that makes me feel like a young schoolgirl instead of a grown ass adult.

"I think my stupid, useless, pathetic heart fell in love with him," Lily says.

My eyes rapidly find her. Color me shocked by her admission. I want to check my ears to make sure I heard her correctly. "Are we talking about the same person? *Aspen,* Aspen?" I point at him, and at that exact moment, he mimics humping something against the pool table.

Lily shrieks, reaching across the table and slapping my hand. "Oh my god, Veronica! You can't just point at him." She shrinks down in the booth, pulling her jacket collar up to hide behind. It's a bit over dramatic considering Aspen hasn't even looked our way since we started the conversation, but I decide not to tell her that.

"Sorry," I mumble. "But are we seriously talking about the same human being? You're in love with *Aspen?*"

"Yes!" She groans and then, "Don't make me feel worse about it than I already do, Veronica. He's gross. Incredibly ugly. No sense of humor at all. My heart will come to its senses soon, I'm sure." Lily sits up and throws her hair over her shoulder. "Anywhooo…tell me about you and my brother. Because I'm not too dumb to notice the way you two have been staring at each other like two love-sick puppies."

It's my turn to gasp, anxiously looking at Maverick to make sure he didn't overhear what Lily just said. He's all the way across the bar, but I still need the reassurance. I don't need him getting any ideas about us.

"I don't know what you're talking about." I take a drink of my beer. It's lukewarm at this point, but it sends alcohol through my bloodstream, which is all I need. My face grimaces at the bitter aftertaste.

"Look, I've known Maverick my whole life," she says.

"Obviously. You're twins."

"Could you not interrupt me? Thanks. Back to what I was saying." She leans forward, propping her elbows on the table. "Since Maverick and I are *twins*, I've seen him with other girls— well, mostly just Selma. Don't get me wrong, Maverick loved Selma, he always will. But I told her for the past year that they didn't belong together as a couple. The way he is around you is different, Veronica. It's different. And the verdict is still out if that different is good or bad because I know you're fucked up and have your own shit you're dealing with. But he's different with you. It's obvious the two of you have hooked up."

I stare at her, my mind turning over her words.

She doesn't allow me to stew in silence though, because she begins to talk again. "Which reminds me, I need to have the obligatory talk with you, that if you break my brother's heart, I will have to do something to make your pretty face not so pretty anymore. And I can throw a punch just as well as I can refuse to fall in love with my brother's best friend. So, let's not get to that point. Got it?"

"Trust me, I have no intentions on having Maverick's heart enough to break it." I look over at him and find his eyes on me. It sends shivers down my body. Part of me wants to ditch our friends and go back to our place so I can feel his eyes on me in private.

Lily hums, her eyes looking at Maverick and Aspen as well. "I don't think that's going to be an option if you keep going down the road you're on, so you need to make a decision. Allow someone to care for you again or leave. Because the way Maverick is looking at you right now is not a look that says the two of you can stay fuck buddies without feelings getting involved."

Lenny drops two more beers off at our table, which I gladly take. When I look at her again, I tell her, "Maverick knows where I stand on relationships and feelings and all that bullshit."

"He might *know*, but he might think he can change your mind."

"I don't know what to do, Lily. Things are different with him. I feel less shitty when he's around. The way he looks at me makes me feel like maybe I'm not as horrible of a human being as I thought. Because a person like me has to have some kind of redeeming quality about them to deserve to be looked at like that. But I've been there before—you know that—and the last time I felt anything close to this, it ended in me losing the one person who made me feel that way. I can't go through that again." I stare at the dull colors of the beer label. My long, manicured nail picks at the peeling label.

I think back to the time I drunkenly told Lily about my past. It was right after I came clean to Maverick. It just kind of slipped out to her. Something about the Morrison twins makes me spill out like paint on a white canvas. When she didn't judge me, even after I'd told her about my mistakes, it made me finally view her as a friend—probably the best friend I have.

Lily snaps her fingers, gaining my attention once again. "You are going to listen to me, Veronica, and you are going to listen carefully. You fucked up. We all have. You went through a traumatic experience. It's obviously something you're going to have to cope with for the rest of your life, but it wasn't all your fault. And you have to stop using Connor's death as an excuse to avoid being vulnerable again."

"I'm not using his death as an excuse."

"Oh, *please*. That's exactly what you're doing. You're so scared to lose someone again that you hide behind this façade that you're trying to protect others from you when in reality *you* are the one that needs to be protected."

I scoff. "Shut up, Lily. You have no idea what you're talking about."

"You're right. I know nothing." The look she gives me from across the table dares me to continue to argue with her.

"There's a consequence for loving me. You wouldn't understand," I tell her.

"The only consequence of loving you is that you're too damn scared of being loved."

"You're one to talk. How long have you been in love with Aspen? Because I'm guessing it's been a long time and isn't some new event."

Lily's eyes defiantly narrow at me. I know I've pissed her off —it's what I do. I'd rather lash out at someone than maybe show them how I really feel.

"Don't try and pin this on me," she says. "I confronted my feelings. I'm not the one parading around pretending they're doing the world a favor by just messing around with guys instead of accepting the fact they've been hurt."

We stare at each other for another long moment before she grabs her purse and scoots out of the booth, leaving me alone with my thoughts.

My eyes follow her as she says goodbye to Maverick. He holds her elbow as she whispers something in his ear. Whatever it is, his eyes snap to me. She continues to tell him something while he leans a hip on the old pool table. His eyes stay on me the whole time. When Lily's done, she gives her brother a hug, Aspen the middle finger, and me one more piercing look before she leaves.

35

MAVERICK

"What did you and Lily talk about tonight?" I ask Veronica as we lie in bed after our second round of sex.

We both came home from Lenny's ready to taste each other. As soon as we ditched Aspen in the living room and made it to the basement, we were all over each other. We didn't even have time to make it into her room before I was inside of her.

We fucked against the basement wall. We were clawing at each other's clothes, unable to strip them off fast enough. I had to keep my lips on hers to keep her from making too much noise so Aspen wouldn't hear us.

Now we're in bed, cuddling and talking.

I haven't been able to get Lily's words out of my head. When my sister was leaving Lenny's, she told me to confront Veronica about my feelings. It caught me off guard. I hadn't realized I had such strong feelings for her until Lily pointed it out to me. I was probably in denial because I knew they wouldn't be accepted well by her.

As my mind races, I hold her head to my chest, letting my fingers run through the long strands of her hair. My clothes are somewhere between her bed and the basement stairs. She's wearing a T-shirt of mine that she's worn to bed every night for the last week.

"Oh nothing," she mumbles against my chest nonchalantly.

As I've gotten to know Veronica more, I've seen different sides to her. Where she's bitter and blunt with others, she's quiet and timid behind closed doors. There's no doubt in my mind that she's jaded and that attitude of hers will never go away, but she doesn't try as hard to seem so bitchy when it's just us. She's just her—the her I've come to know I like maybe a little too much.

"It didn't appear that way. When I looked over at the two of you, it seemed like you were talking about something that had you both heated." My fingers are still playing with her hair. I wish I could see her face right now, but it's tucked into the crook of my neck.

"You might've misread things. Aspen was being weird next to you. Maybe his gyrating hips had you excited."

"Veronica, can we have a serious conversation for two seconds without you changing the subject?"

She begins to trace along my stomach. Her bright pink nail inches down my abs. Another contradiction of hers. I envisioned her as a woman who would wear black nail polish, maybe something duller, but I've only seen her wear girly colors.

"It was nothing. I don't want to talk about it, Maverick." The resignation in her voice is very clear to me, but I decide to ignore it.

Now that Lily has planted this seed in my head, I can't get it to go away. I need to tell her how I feel, even if it will start the fight I know is bound to happen.

"Well, I do," I say softly.

"We had a conversation about you. Happy?" She sighs against my neck. Her breath is warm on my skin and I want to bury myself inside her, but I know I'll feel even worse if I don't have the balls to confront her about us.

"What kind of conversation?" Her finger stills on my bare chest.

I'm confident she can feel the thrumming of my heart underneath it.

She lifts her head, looking at me with those big blue eyes that convey innocence even though I know she is anything but.

"She doesn't want me to break your heart. Lily is protective of you. I get it. I told her there's no possible way you and I will ever be in the position where I could break your heart."

A pit forms in my stomach. I don't know if she's just oblivious to how I feel about her or if she's still in that much denial. I'm betting it's the latter, which pisses me off.

"Would it be that bad if I did have feelings for you?" I couldn't keep the question from leaving my mouth for another moment longer. The more I try to put her pieces together, the more I realize I'm falling for all the individual pieces that make her. And now that she's let me in to see the whole picture, I can't look away.

"I told you, Maverick. You can't have feelings for me." Veronica sits up, her blonde hair creating a blanket around her face as she looks down at me.

The fear is clear as day in her eyes. She wants to flee, I know it. But I will stand my ground until she decides to run for the hills, all while hoping she won't.

I pull myself up in the bed, taking part of the sheet so it still covers my naked body. "You can't just tell someone not to have feelings for you. It doesn't fucking work like that. You told me not to fall for you, and I appreciate the warning, but I'm telling you it didn't work because I'm sitting in front of you with feelings for you and I'm tired of the bullshit. This thing we've had for the last month has turned into something more than I thought it would. I'm falling for you and there's no warning you can give me to stop it from happening because it's already begun."

Her head starts to frantically shake. Her small hands pull at the bottom of my T-shirt she's wearing, wringing it to give her hands something to do. "No, this isn't happening."

Dread begins to pool its way through my body. It starts in the pit of my stomach and oozes out into every single part of me. The look on her face makes it apparent that she isn't letting go of the silly thought that no one should love her again.

My hand reaches out to touch her, my body craving to feel her, even if it's a small amount. Right as my fingertip is about to graze her thigh, she scoots away from me, so far down the bed that there's no way I can touch her unless I move.

"I'm sorry. I shouldn't be, but I am. I didn't have the intention of wanting you. I really didn't."

"Don't do this, Maverick. You don't know what you're saying."

I shake my head at her in disbelief. "Looking back, you've been collecting small pieces of me this whole time. And it was wrong. I didn't even realize I was doing it before, because I was so committed to Selma. But now that I'm not pretending anymore, I can say I've been handing myself over to you, hoping to maybe get a damn scrap back."

Veronica steps off the bed and begins to pace back and forth.

It's ironic, because as I throw the covers off me to look for my boxers, I accidentally knock a picture she painted of Connor off the nightstand.

Connor. A man I haven't met, but a man that still holds her heart captive. More than that, holds her soul captive, because neither her head nor her heart can get past what happened to him.

I search for my boxers, finding them on the floor in front of her closet. My mouth continues to ramble on as I shove both my legs through the holes. "Now that I think about it, it's pathetic how I've been begging this whole time for *something* from you. Whether it be your thoughts, your feelings, your past, or even a small fucking piece of your heart. I was begging for any of it, *all of it*, even if it was the smallest piece. Anytime I feel that maybe I finally have something from you, even if it's broken and jagged and bleeding, you pull it out from me so fast I land on my ass. But I stand up and ask for more again and again and *again*. Just when I think I'm lucky enough to have that from you, you slap it out of my hand with your dismissive comments and attitude."

"It's the sex. You'll get over it once you aren't inside me all the time. You'll find you were attracted to my body, not the pieces of me within it."

"Don't degrade yourself like that, Veronica. It's childish. I'm an adult who can navigate my own feelings. I could never be buried inside you again yet still feel this way."

"You don't know that." She opens the door and stomps out of her room like a damn child.

Even though I'm still in nothing but my underwear, I follow her, nowhere near done with this conversation.

36

VERONICA

I'm a few steps out into the living area of the basement when Maverick comes charging in behind me.

"For fuck's sake, Veronica. What do I need to do to prove to you that I'm not just spewing shit out of my mouth because I want to sleep with you? Because I'll do it."

I turn around and face him. "I need you to keep your promise. The promise that this wouldn't be more than just sex. You promised!"

"I didn't promise a thing. I remember it very clearly. This has never been *just sex* for me. Is that really what I am to you? Just another guy to get you off? Because I refuse to believe that."

"Well believe it, Maverick." My hands are on my hips as I speak the words to him. While I stand in nothing but his T-shirt —the T-shirt I refused to return because it smells like him and I relish in the comfort it gives me.

His hands fly up in the air as an exasperated sigh escapes his lips. "You make it hard to fall for you, you know that?"

"That's the point! You weren't supposed to feel anything. I may be a lot of things in this world, but one thing I haven't been with you is vague. I've told you from the beginning that I don't want anyone falling for me. Not since Connor."

"Connor isn't a part of this, Veronica. Don't you get that? He's not here anymore and I'm sorry. I'm so fucking *sorry*. I wish you didn't have to lose him like that, but he's been gone for years now. You need to let yourself move on. How am I supposed to fall in love with you when you're still in love with a ghost?"

"Stop talking about Connor." I cover my ears, the walls beginning to cave in around me. My past and present are colliding in a vicious moment I'm not prepared for. Hearing Connor's name come from Maverick's mouth causes me to feel too much at once.

"That's the problem. You have to acknowledge what happened to him. You have to acknowledge that you loved him, that the love wasn't enough to keep him alive, and I'm sorry. The fact of the matter is that no matter how much you love someone—and I mean *really* fucking love them, mind, body and soul—you can't keep them alive when their time comes. He died. He died and he's not coming back. My feelings are so strong for you I would do anything in the world to bring him back to you. Just so I don't have to see your grief. But I can't. And *you* can't keep using his death as your excuse to never love again. You have to fall out of love with a ghost. Come back to reality. Come to *me*." His voice cracks by the end.

The look on his face is serious, his eyes pleading. "I think you're scared. And I think you blame yourself for Connor's death because I think it's easier for you to pretend that there's a reason, a cause behind his death other than to simply admit that sometimes people die, Veronica. Sometimes people die and it's horrible and tragic and I wish it wasn't. But they die. And it isn't anyone's fault. Could things have been different if the two of you weren't in the water? Yes. Yes, they one hundred percent could have been, but you both made a choice. It isn't anyone's fault. It's just life being life.

"You and Connor could have never gotten in the water and he could have died the next day in a car accident. Or he could have lived to be a hundred years old. We just don't fucking know. We have to live, and we have to live every single day. And god damn it, Veronica, if I don't want to live each day with you. I don't fucking care what that means. I don't care if you think I'll get hurt or that you'll destroy me. Because I would rather die tomorrow knowing I got the girl that's holding my heart in her hands than die seventy years from now after living with *what ifs* for the rest of my life.

"You think you're selfish and I think you're selfless. You think there are consequences for falling in love with you and I think they're benefits. You think you destroy what you love but I think you heal it. Because you've healed me. You've taught me what it is to love someone, unconditionally, and to love them for who they are, not for who you want them to be.

"You're scared, and baby, I get why you're scared—I do. I'm scared, too. I don't want to lose you, but I would rather have you for a little while than never at all. I would rather have any moment life will give me with you than play it safe. It's scary to know there's no rhyme or reason why infants get cancer, why people abuse animals, why parents leave their children, why people fight wars they want no part in. There's absolutely none. We can't make sense of why things happen the way they do, but we also can't blame ourselves for every hideous thing in this world. Because there's a lot. And one person can't handle it all. So, I need you to stop blaming yourself for Connor's death and realize that people just die because they do."

Part of me understands what he's saying. I know I need to leave the pain I associate with Connor in the past and move on, keeping only the happy memories of the two of us. I have to let go of what happened to him and forgive myself, because Maverick is right. Connor's gone, but I'm still here. And I know, with every part of me, that if there's something beyond this messed up world we live in that allows Connor to be looking down on me, he'd be disappointed by my actions.

A large part of me understands all of it. That part of me wants to drop this fight with Maverick and run into his arms and tell him even though it was quick and unexpected, I have strong feelings for him, too. I desperately want to tell him he isn't alone in this.

But I'm terrified.

I'm absolutely petrified that I will ruin Maverick somehow. It's what I seem to do. So, even though my limbs desperately want to wrap around him, I hold back. I hurt him more—to protect him. "It was just sex for me, Maverick."

His body jerks like I punched him in the chest. He runs a hand through his hair, pulling at it while he looks at the ceiling. I've hurt him so much he can't even look me in the eye.

I stand next to the old couch we explored each other on in nothing but his T-shirt. My hands play with the fabric at the bottom, twisting it. With every twist of the shirt, I feel my heart twist inside of me. I try to think of something else to say to him, something we won't be able to come back from, but he beats me to it.

"Destroy what destroys you." He recites the words that are tattooed on my body. The words that his fingers—and tongue—have traced many times.

But this time, it doesn't give me butterflies. Now, all the butterflies inside me are dead. My stomach feels heavy, full with the weight of his words.

His gaze finds mine and I do something right for the first time in my life. I look him in the eyes and allow him to say what he needs to. It'll kill me later to think of this anguish and regret on his face, but I know whatever he's about to say is important to him. So, even though it kills me to look into those ocean eyes, I do. For him.

"The first time I read those words on your body, I was confused," he says. "When you told me love destroyed you, I couldn't comprehend why you would want to destroy it. The ironic thing here is that you told me from the beginning that you wanted to destroy love, but I didn't listen. I didn't want to believe you. And I want to feel shitty about it, but I don't. Because even after all this, Veronica, it's *you* I feel bad for. This will hurt me for a long time, but I'm strong enough to know that love *heals*. It doesn't destroy. Your pain, *that's* what destroys.

"I thought maybe if you allowed me to love you, I could heal you. But I was wrong. You're too busy with your illusions. I feel bad for you. It's easy to let the pain in, to let the pain win. But you know what's harder? To love. Because loving someone —even if there might be consequences—takes strength. I have that strength, but I can't say the same for you. Love didn't destroy you, Veronica. Pain did. Insecurities did. Guilt did. Love is the only thing that can heal you, but you're too scared to heal. So, go destroy somebody else's heart."

He doesn't say it with malice.

I know he's done when he walks up to me and presses a lingering kiss to my forehead. A gesture that obliterates every piece of my heart. The pieces of me he put together have just shattered all over again, but this time into even more pieces than before. Maverick keeps his warm lips against my head long enough for me to almost ask him to stay.

But before my words can come out, and before he can see the tears fall from my eyes, he walks up the stairs and leaves me there—silently sobbing, too scared to even watch him walk away.

The slamming of the door opens up the flood gates of my heart.

I fall to the ground, the sobs taking over me.

37

MAVERICK

HOURS LATER, the knot in my stomach still hasn't disappeared. I lie in bed, staring at the ceiling, my mind retracing every step that led me here. The sun is now peeking through my window. It reminds me of yesterday morning—when I woke up with Veronica in my arms. I was happy. She was giggling, fucking *giggling*. Her guard was down and it was beautiful.

Twenty-four hours later and things have drastically changed.

I don't know if I'll ever wake up with her in my arms again, but I don't regret telling her how I feel. I do, however, regret the way I foolishly ignored her warnings not to fall for her.

I wanted to prove her wrong.

In my heart, I thought we could be different.

I thought I could teach her how to forgive herself, to put herself out there again—that she was worth it. But all I taught her was that she couldn't even be *just friends* with a guy, because our friendship turned into more—a *more* I couldn't come back from.

I could never look at her again as just a friend.

Once I put the puzzle of her together, I realized I couldn't settle for pieces anymore. I needed the whole picture or nothing at all.

She chose nothing.

A car door slams. It sends my body into action. My feet hit

the soft carpet before I can really think about it. I reach the window, my eyes taking in a sight that sends the final blow to my heart.

Veronica, in front of her car, her back facing my window as she shoves a pink duffle bag into her front seat. She's got on those boots that caught my attention the day I met her. Who knew those same boots would be the boots she'd run away from me in?

Because it's obvious by the bag that now sits in her passenger side that she's leaving.

She's running.

And even though I could run out and try to change her mind, my feet stay planted. I'm tired—*exhausted*—of chasing her. There were only so many times she could tell me I was nothing but sex to her before I started to believe her.

I'm still confident it meant more to her, but I won't continue to try to make her admit that. If she wants to convince herself we were just two people having fun this whole time, then I'll let her believe it.

Veronica climbs into her car and slams her door shut. I watch from the window as she looks up at the spot where I stand. My blinds are drawn—I know she can't see me—so I allow myself to be fascinated with her one last time.

She swipes underneath her eyes, making it obvious that she's crying. It seems like two hours, but it's probably only two minutes that she stares at the window.

A piece of my pathetic heart hopes she's changing her mind about leaving—about us.

But her car engine starts, proving me wrong yet again.

Veronica looks up at my window one more time before she starts to reverse down the driveway.

Her rearview lights disappear in the early morning sun, taking what's left of my heart along with her.

38

VERONICA

"Done." I click the green button to turn in my last final of the semester before slamming my laptop shut. This earns me a look from my mother from across the long table.

She's flipping through a magazine, mumbling judgments of different celebrities as she does so. "You know you're very fortunate your father could pull enough strings to allow you to finish this semester fully online." Her tongue sticks out to lick her finger as she continues to rifle through the pages.

She's right. After my confrontation with Maverick, I fled. I came back to South Carolina. That week break turned into a month. Once I was home, I couldn't muster up the courage to return to Kansas. Any time I thought I could face Maverick, I remembered the disappointed look on his face as he watched me from his bedroom window. I could barely see him through his blinds, but I saw enough to know I'd let him down.

I was always letting people down, and I couldn't go back there just to do it again.

It took a lot of begging—and lies—to get my father to contact the dean of my college. They have mutual friends, so the dean agreed to let me finish the rest of my classes online. And for the last month, I've been hiding. I never thought I'd run back to the place I had initially run *from*, but my life is quite ironic. I'd rather face my past here than face my present in Kansas.

My heart still misses Maverick. When I'm alone at night, I cry. I cry because I destroyed the *one* good thing in my life because I was too damn scared to have him destroy me instead.

I haven't heard from anyone on campus except for Lily and she is freaking persistent. I hadn't been in South Carolina for a full *day* before she started blowing up my phone. At first, her voicemails and texts were all angry. She even cussed me out via video using a pretty filter on Snapchat.

But then she started to give me random updates. Updates on her volleyball team. Updates on her relationship with Aspen—or lack thereof. Updates on her skincare routine.

Her updates on Maverick were the ones I craved the most.

Her texts that assured me he was still single. Her texts that told me what he was doing. Her texts that made me feel like shit because she told me he was doing well.

He's doing fine, and I'm barely getting by here at home.

I miss him.

I miss him so fucking much, and I don't know what to do about it.

"Veronica?"

I look up to find my mom watching me with a curious stare. I have no idea what she was saying before I got lost in my thoughts, so I adjust my position in the uncomfortable chair and wait for her to repeat herself.

But she doesn't, so I say, "What, Mom?"

"I was asking if you've decided yet if you're going back to Kansas or not when the spring semester starts. It's silly that we're still paying for that house on campus when you aren't even there. I think it's time you decide what you want to do next." Her hand reaches across the table and rests on top of mine—a comfort.

I stare down at her nude fingernails. She's been wearing the same color of nail polish for as long as I can remember.

Before this recent retreat home, I didn't let my mom touch me. But over the last month, we've formed a better relationship. For some reason, she hasn't pressured me about why I came back. And I've appreciated it. It's helped us grow closer, *together* —close enough that I don't back away from her touch anymore.

I let out a long sigh, wishing I had an honest answer for her. The more I think about it, the more I want to return to Kansas. To go back to the place that had started to feel like *home*, a fresh start for me. But another part of me—a large part—worries what I might do if I see Maverick again. And I know I *would* see him if I go back there. That campus is so small, there's no way around it.

"I don't know, Mom." My words cut off as I try to come up with the best answer and fall short.

She purses her pink lips. I can tell she wants to pester me with questions—questions I won't answer. Her cold hand squeezes mine. "I support whatever decision you make, Veronica. I hope you know that."

I'm nodding my head at her when my father walks into our large kitchen and says, "Are my two favorite ladies ready to go?" He's fiddling with his cuff links as he walks toward us.

We're all ready to go to a charity function at their country club. A function that benefits the charity Connor's parents created in his name, providing free ocean safety classes for the youth in our area.

I can't lie and say I'm not nervous to face his parents for the first time. But it's something I need to do.

When I came home, I started seeing my therapist again.

After cussing him out a few times, and sobbing—or both at the same time—he finally got me to realize that, for me to heal and move on from Connor's death, I had to face Mr. and Mrs. Liams.

So, here I am, standing in a black evening gown ready to address my past. My palms are sweating, and the slippery fabric of my dress doesn't help when I try to wipe them off. I feel like I could throw up at any moment as I climb into the black limo my father rented for the night.

When I get inside the sleek vehicle, I slide in right next to my mom. There's enough room with my dad across from us for me to be in my own space. At twenty, I still need my mother's calm composure in a time like this.

She doesn't hesitate to take my hand in hers. Her fingers squeeze mine tightly as the limo pulls away from our driveway.

"We probably haven't said this enough to you, Veronica," my father begins, his thumb flicking over his gold cuff links, "but we are proud of you. So proud." His blue eyes—the same as mine—stare at me as he enunciates every word he's saying. "You've been through a lot and we wish you would've let us shoulder some of the pain you've endured, but even all alone, you've come out the other side. It takes strength to go through something that's meant to break you and only come out stronger. We're proud of you."

My mom nods her head next to me. "You're so strong. Please don't forget that." She runs a hand over my styled hair; the hair that two women had come hours ago to do, as well as my mom's.

My long, blonde strands fall down my shoulders in loose curls. I have one side tucked behind my ear, showing off a pair of diamond earrings. All I can do is nod my head, pulling my red bottom lip to chew on as I remind myself not to cry. I hate that I was weak and ran home, but I have to admit, it's been nice spending time with my parents again.

I'm done playing the part of a spoiled brat. I just want to be *Veronica* again. A little bit spoiled, a little bit bitchy. But I don't want to be a brat anymore for the sake of scaring people away.

My stomach lurches when the limo comes to a stop in front of the club. The ride went by too fast. I start to choke on the air in the limo that smells like perfume and cologne.

I'm not ready to go in there.

"You've got this, Veronica Rose Cunningham," my mom says. "I promise you that the Liams are excited to see you. I think this will go so much better than you're imagining." My mom stares into my eyes for a moment longer before she takes my dad's outstretched hand and steps out of the limo.

I release a long burst of air, my mind giving me an internal pep talk. My lips spread in a plastered fake smile before I extend my high-heeled clad foot from the limo and get out.

My eyes take in the scene before me.

Holy fuck. Pray for me.

39

VERONICA

I LOOK up at the stairs that lead to the country club I've been coming to since I was in diapers. The railings are decorated in garland, reminding me that Christmas is in a week.

I follow my mom and dad up the stairs without thinking too hard about it. I'm too focused on taking in my surroundings. There's a huge banner of Connor's face next to a person with a clipboard at the entrance. My throat starts to close with emotion as I stare at Connor's smiling face. He's standing in front of the ocean. The same ocean we've all played in our whole lives.

The same ocean that took him from me.

My eyes avert from the banner, I can't look at it for another second without bursting into tears. The man at the door runs his finger down the clipboard in his hand, looking for our names. Once he finds them, he gives us a smile and motions for us to walk in.

I don't even know where to look first when we walk through the entrance. The club has been decorated beautifully. It seems like we're in a winter wonderland. White and blue decorations fill almost every space. White for winter, blue for the ocean and the main color of the charity in Connor's name.

It's so beautiful it makes me gasp. I'm aimlessly following my mom to our table when I spot the Liams from across the room, and my feet stop. I don't realize a woman's behind me until her champagne sloshes all over her. The nasty words she mumbles don't even register in my mind because I'm too busy staring at the parents of the boy I used to love.

The boy who broke my heart when he died.

The boy whose heart I broke seconds before he died.

Even though the ballroom is huge, I feel suffocated. The sound of blood pumping through my body rushes in my ears—reminding me of the waves that stole Connor from me.

I want to turn around so badly. I want to slip off these heels and run to the limo, to escape from the memories swooshing through my brain, threatening to suck me under with them.

The woman next to me is still cleaning herself up, whispering things I'm sure she means to insult me with, when Connor's mom's eyes find me from across the room.

I'm pinned to my spot.

I can't fucking move.

Oh my fuck.

She's looking at me.

She's—why is she smiling at me?

Before I can panic and sprint out of here like my ass is on fire, she starts to walk toward me. Her navy-blue gown billows around her as she tugs on her husband's elbow. Connor's dad says something to the man they were talking to, his eyes traveling in the direction his wife points to.

My direction.

His face is unreadable when his eyes land on me.

I don't even have the time to think of an excuse to high-tail it out of here before they're standing right in front of me.

I watch in horror as Connor's mom—Maria—reaches her slender arms toward me and pulls me in for a hug without warning. I'm still trying to process what the hell is happening when her arms wrap tightly around my shoulders.

"I'm so happy to you, sweetie," Maria says into my hair. Her hand pets the back of my head a few times.

I can smell her. She smells like vanilla. Connor did, too. Their whole house did.

It brings back so many memories.

"I'm happy to see you, too, Maria." The words are out of

my mouth before I can even think about it. I look at Connor's dad—Kenneth—as I add, "I'm sorry it's taken so long."

Kenneth nods his head at me, putting his hand on the small of Maria's back.

Maria pulls away from our hug, her small hands finding both of my cheeks. "It took the amount of time you needed. Don't apologize for that." She kisses my cheek before completely pulling away from me.

The three of us stand there awkwardly. Well, I at least feel awkward. I can't tell if they do or not.

Someone steps up to our small group just as I'm about to say something to fill the silence between us. The Liams both nod their heads at something the guest says before looking back at me when the person walks away.

"The auction is about to start," Maria says, "but I would love to catch up with you soon, Veronica—if you'd be up to it." A pause and then, "Would you like to come over for tea soon?"

I nod, too overcome with emotion to say anything else.

The million times I've envisioned seeing the Liams again, I never *once* imagined them being so forgiving. So nice. So true to how I remembered them before we lost Connor. I thought Maria would scream at me. I thought I'd see disappointment or resentment written all over Kenneth's face.

But here they are, giving me hugs and asking if I'll come over for tea.

"I would very much like that," I finally respond, swiping at a stray tear that's managed to escape my eye.

Maria stares at it for a moment, a look of contemplation on her face. "Great," she says, giving me a small squeeze on the hand before she and Kenneth walk away to entertain the rest of their guests.

I'm processing everything that just happened as I walk to the table my mother and father are seated at. My mom swipes at her eyes with a napkin. It makes my heart jump inside my chest. I don't realize until *right now* why she's been so insistent that I understand the Liams aren't full of resentment, the way I imagined them to be in my head.

"Thank you for doing that, honey," my mom says, putting

down the napkin and straightening her back to appear composed. And then she mouths, "I'm *so proud* of you."

People all around us begin to take their seats. After a few minutes, the lights dim and Connor's parents take the stage.

"Thank you all for coming tonight," Kenneth says as he puts an arm around Maria's waist. "It means the world to us that so many of you consistently come out to support Connor's Ocean, the charity we founded in honor of our oldest son."

A slideshow begins behind the two of them.

A photo of Connor and his two brothers appears first.

Then comes Connor and his whole family.

Next is Connor—*and me.*

My heart breaks all over again as I'm taken back to that very moment with him.

Pictures from classes the charity has hosted on ocean safety show up after that.

"We lost our son to the ocean years ago, but we didn't want that to scare us away from it. From the beauty of the ocean. Many of us have been on the beach for as long as we can remember, and we didn't want to fear it due to what happened to Connor. Because our son—" Kenneth pauses, swallowing, his voice breaking on Connor's name. "Our son made a mistake. Our mission is to prevent someone else's child from making that same mistake. Our efforts have helped put on more than two thousand ocean safety classes since we founded this charity. That's over thirty thousand people we've reached, teaching them about the dangers of the ocean and how to be safe while in or around it."

He pauses again, looking over at his wife who's somehow smiling next to him.

Pictures are still appearing behind them, but I'm too focused on Kenneth's words. Too devastated to see more photos of Connor's beautiful and missed face.

"Auctions, like the one we're about to begin, allow us the funds to hold more safety classes. We have a goal to fill more lifeguard positions next year, to add that extra safety precaution on the beaches we love. So, before I talk all your ears off, let's begin the auction." Kenneth hands the microphone over to Maria.

I lean closer in my seat, already hanging on every word she's yet to say.

"Every item you see here tonight has been donated by very generous donors. Some of you have already bid on items we laid out in the grand room for your viewing. We appreciate how much money you've already donated, just on those items alone. Now, we will present you with many more items in effort to help us fund our wishes for the upcoming year. I will explain the items up for auction, and if you'd like to bid, please hold up your paddle." Maria fixes the train of her dress and faces the huge monitor behind her.

"First up is an all-expenses paid trip to Breckenridge, Colorado. This includes a five-night stay in a ski in, ski out cabin. Air fare is included. Bids will begin at two thousand dollars." Maria looks out into the audience as paddles are raised all over the room.

For the next forty-five minutes, I'm struck with awe as a ton of money is raised. They've auctioned off trips, meat, experiences, gifts, TVs, and so much more. At first, I tried to calculate how much money they'd raised thus far for Connor's Ocean, but eventually the number got too high for me to keep track of.

My mom and I are chatting about the dress one of the winners has on when Kenneth goes back on the stage. He stands next to his wife as she smiles out at the audience.

"The next group of items are very special to us," Maria begins. "They were brought to us by a very generous donor. He told us we could do with the items as we liked, that he felt we deserved them and would want to see them. He had mentioned how important it was to him, that if we could find it in our hearts to part with any of them, that they be auctioned off for money for the charity in Connor's name. While there were two very special pieces we kept for ourselves, the rest we want to share with you. The donor has requested to remain anonymous, but his one wish is that if you buy one of these pieces, that you buy them with the intent to fully appreciate them. He was very firm that they couldn't be simply a *talking piece* at your dinners."

There was a collective laugh heard in the ballroom. And then, "So, please, keep that in mind before you raise your paddle."

Men in tuxedos begin to push carts into the room with velvet blankets hung over them. There are four carts on the stage now. The audience is silent as we wait to see what's been donated. I'm on the edge of my seat. I can tell, by the way Kenneth and Maria are both beaming on stage, that whatever has been donated is very special to them.

I feel so much anticipation as Maria kindly asks the men to pull off the covers.

The audience gasps as the paintings come into full view.

I gasp, too—probably loudest of all.

Because on stage are four of *my* paintings.

The paintings I made after telling Maverick my story.

The same exact paintings Maverick bought from Clementine's.

A sob breaks free from my chest when I realize what he's done. When I *see* his love for me, selflessly auctioned off in the name of my first love.

"This collection is called *Imperfections* and was done by a very talented young artist," Maria says.

Even though I'm seated in the middle of the crowded room, Maria's eyes find mine. She softly smiles at me and I can't help but return a pain-stricken smile back to her.

"Bidding will start at ten thousand for the one on the far left," she states confidently.

People raise their paddles enthusiastically as they auction off each of my paintings. I don't even realize I'm clutching my mother's hand like a lifeline as numbers are thrown out that are way larger than I could have ever expected.

Tears fall freely from my eyes as I witness my work raise more than one hundred thousand dollars for Connor's Ocean.

My paintings.

I was so pissed at Maverick for buying them.

Now, I don't know how I could ever repay him.

He gave me the greatest gift of all. Maverick had been so adamant that he didn't want these paintings on some rich person's wall, but instead of keeping them all for himself, he donated them to charity.

To *Connor's* charity.

My hand goes to my mouth when it all clicks together.

This man.

I love him.

Oh my god. I actually love him.

The realization makes me push my chair out from the table.

I need air.

I need it fast.

40

VERONICA

"I can't explain to you how happy I am that you chose to come visit." Maria holds the front door open to their home, gesturing for me to come inside.

I stand in the middle of their entryway, looking around the house I used to be so familiar with. It's a lot smaller than the house I grew up in, but that's why I always loved it. It had charm without being flashy and in your face.

It's been over a week since the charity function. Over a week of me crying, smiling, laughing, and wishing I could call Maverick to thank him. I have yet to talk to him, though. After talking with my therapist, I agreed with him that I needed to talk with the Liams more before I attempted to move on to anything else.

So, here I am—standing in the Liams' entryway, petrified of how this might go down.

They were nothing but kind to me at the charity function, but that doesn't mean my anxiety isn't at an all-time high. For me to leave this conversation feeling like I can move on, I have to tell them the whole story. From my lips. And they can do with that information as they please.

I would understand if they never wanted to see me again.

But for the first time in forever, I have hope. Hope that they can forgive me for the exact thing I haven't been able to forgive myself for. For the part I played in their son's tragic death.

Footsteps echo through the house. They come from upstairs, where Connor's younger twin brothers must be getting into trouble. Kenneth barks something at the two of them. Giggling is heard soon after.

Maria and I share a smile. She leads me to their kitchen, where teacups and cookies are already placed on the table. "Please sit, Veronica," Maria says softly, giving me her warm smile as she pulls a tea kettle off the stove.

This would probably be a bad time to confess to her that I hate tea, but I sucked it up for her when I was dating Connor and I will suck it up today as well.

I mutter a *thank you* as she fills my cup with piping hot tea. Steam wafts out the top in soft spirals. After she pours herself a cup and is putting the kettle back on the stove, I put about five spoonfuls of sugar in my cup behind her back.

We sit in silence for a few agonizing moments. It's just long enough for my heart to start hammering against my chest.

"Your paintings are so beautiful."

It's not what I expect her to say, so I choke on the hot tea that's halfway down my throat. After coughing for a minute straight, I'm finally able to respond. "Thank you so much, Maria. To be honest, I don't even know what to say."

Maria gives me a beaming smile. "Thank you works just fine. Please know I mean it. The two pieces we kept of Connor, I'll never be able to thank you enough for. They are so special to us."

"Oh, please don't thank me." I look down at my teacup, too uncomfortable to look her in the eye at the moment. "I would never have had the nerve to show you those, if they hadn't been donated. I just——"

I suck a deep breath in, trying to come up with a way to start this conversation. "I just didn't think you and Kenneth would want anything from me after everything that happened."

"Will you look at me?" Maria's hand reaches across the white table and places it on my wrist.

I stare at my tea for a few moments longer before I get the

courage to look her in the eye again. I don't see any resentment on her face. There's no hate or disappointment. I just see a face that is calm. Loving. Understanding. I still feel like I don't deserve it, but I can't turn away from her kindness.

"Kenneth and I never blamed you, Veronica. Do you understand that?" Her small hand tightens on my wrist to get her point across.

I can feel the lump in my throat start to form. I've needed to hear those words for years, but I still can't fully believe them.

How can they not blame me?

They still might when they hear the whole story from my mouth.

"You don't know everything," I manage to choke out.

Maria leans back in her chair while holding her teacup. "Why don't you tell me then?"

I take in a huge deep breath, trying to suck in as much courage as I can. This will be the moment that destroys me or heals me. Her reaction to hearing the truth is what will seal my fate. I can't go on another day with this guilt on my back. But if she can forgive me for the part I played...well, maybe I can get rid of the burden that has sat on my chest for years.

"It was my fault Connor was even in the ocean. We were fighting because I was being dumb. I loved your son, I promise I did—I still do. But, back then, I had a lot of personal things I hadn't worked through." I shake my head and let out a nervous, disgusted laugh. "I needed to fight with him to know he loved me. It was so fucked up."

Her eyes widen, and I add, "Oh my god, I meant *messed up.* I'm sorry for cursing. Anyway, we were fighting. I had conjured this picture in my head where I thought he wanted another girl in our class. I wouldn't let it go. It was so *stupid.*

"We were on the beach, and to get away from me, he walked to the ocean. I followed him. We continued to argue as we both went deeper and deeper into the water. If I hadn't kept egging him on, if I just got out, I know he would've followed me. But I stayed in the water—in those waves—and so did Connor.

"Finally, he hit his breaking point. After a while, I pushed him so far over the edge that he needed to get away from me.

He did that by swimming deeper into the ocean. The next thing I knew I was pulling him onto the shore and he was just…so limp."

I'm talking so fast at this point, emptying all of this off my chest and I can't get rid of it soon enough. I hadn't realized how *badly* I needed her to know everything.

I look her in the eye as tears race out of my eyes. They fall down my cheeks and stick to my chin. "He was so limp, Maria. I tried to bring him back, I swear I did, but it wasn't enough. *I* wasn't enough. I'm so sorry. God, I'm just so freaking sorry."

My throat clogs up at the end.

I can't get anything else out. All I can do is sit there and bawl in front of Connor's mom. I shouldn't even be allowed to grieve. I lost a boyfriend, but she lost her *son*.

I feel guilty for even reacting like this in front of her.

My eyes track a tear that runs down her cheek. Above us, shouting begins again. We both stare at the ceiling for a moment as we hear the twins fight about something in a video game. My eyes are still on the ceiling when Maria begins to speak again.

"When we got the call—that something had happened to Connor—it was the most devastating moment of my life. No mother imagines they'll have to bury their child, but it became my reality. When we got the call, we were out at a little league game for the boys. I dropped to my knees in front of everyone when the officer asked us to come down and identify the body. I lost myself in front of the whole town. Connor was our sweet boy, our first born, I didn't know how to continue on without him and his sense of humor."

At this point we're both crying at her kitchen table, our teacups haphazardly set in front of us, neither of us bothering to touch them.

"When the on-scene paramedics told us what had happened," Maria says, "when they recounted the story you told them, it became the second most devastating moment of my life. Because not only had I lost my son, I was then faced with the fact that you were there when it happened. That must have been such a traumatic experience and I couldn't imagine how you were feeling. I know how much you loved him. Every person we talked to told the same version of the story you just told me, Veronica.

"Except the story they told us had more to it. The fact that you—a tiny girl—had pulled a soaking wet Connor to a safe beach almost all alone. How you did chest compressions on him until your hands bruised. How your eyes were so bloodshot from opening them in the saltwater to look for him. They told us how *hard* you tried to bring him back to us. And I broke down for a second time that day because, even though I had lost a son, and I was absolutely devastated, a girl I loved as my own daughter had just gone through something so horrific. I wanted to reach out to you, but you had to heal in your own way, and I don't blame you *at all* for how you handled things.

"But, Veronica Rose Cunningham, I have to tell you something and I need you to listen very carefully." Maria gives me a determined look, even though tears are still welling up in her eyes. "I never *once* blamed you for what happened to Connor—not once. I know you blame yourself and I wish I could take that burden from you because it isn't one I want you to bear. But please know that every part of me *thanks* you.

"I thank you because you did everything you could to bring him back. And yes, neither one of you should've been in that ocean when you knew the waves were high and that you were near a sandbar. The conditions were perfect for a rip current, but that doesn't mean anyone is to blame or at fault. We've all been in that water at some point when it wasn't safe.

"It was a tragedy that out of the hundred deaths a year there are from rip currents, Connor was one of them. But I will say this again. It isn't your fault, Veronica. It never was. You can't let the guilt from his death continue to eat you alive."

I'm bawling, shaking my head at her.

How is she not blaming me?

It was my fault.

For a few long moments, I refuse to believe she doesn't hold me accountable. But the sincerity in her expression changes my mind.

And I realize she's right; if Connor or I had been paying any attention, we would have known a rip current was likely.

We *were* near the sandbar.

The waves were big.

The ocean was basically *screaming* at us to stay away.

But we both got in the water—both of us.

"Connor wouldn't want you to blame yourself," Maria says. "And we don't want that either. Forgive yourself, Veronica. Please, forgive yourself and live your life the way Connor would have wanted you to. While we don't blame you for what happened to him, I will blame you for wasting your life in an abyss of guilt even after I've told you how we feel. How we don't blame you at all."

Snot falls from my nose as I continue to sob. I've needed to hear these words from Maria's lips for years. I take a deep breath in and, for the first time since I lost Connor, I feel like a weight has been lifted from my shoulders.

Maria comes around the table and pulls me in for a hug. I rest my face in the crook of her neck as we both continue to sob.

It's a moment I will never forget.

A moment of healing. Of moving on. Of going forward.

Finally, we both gain our composure enough to speak.

Maria smiles at me from a splotchy red face. "Would you like to know more about all that we've been able to do with Connor's Ocean?"

I smile at her. A genuine smile. One I feel in every part of my body—even my heart. And my head nods.

41

VERONICA

WE SPEND two hours going through all the things the Liams have been able to do in Connor's name, and it's amazing. I'm in awe, staring in wonder as she shows me everything they've accomplished in the two years Connor's Ocean has been running.

I ask her a million questions, some she answers and some Kenneth answers after he joins us. They've done so many wonderful things in Connor's name and it makes my heart so happy. I wish I could've been part of everything they've done so far, but I take comfort in knowing I'll be part of what they do next.

And she's right when she again reminds me that I needed time to heal. I did need it, but already, I feel like my gaping wound of guilt has started to slowly close.

It feels like healing.

We're flipping through a file folder that holds all the plans for the recent charity function they just hosted. It took *six* whole months for them to plan it. Kenneth shows me the final total of the money they raised and I almost fall out of my chair. They raised over two-hundred thousand dollars. My jaw is hanging open as Maria continues to flip through the folder, continuing on about their future plans for Connor's Ocean.

An envelope falls out and Maria lets out a soft gasp as it

lands on the floor in front of my feet. She quickly bends down to pick it up and says, "This is something you may want to read." Her finger traces over the seam of the envelope before she hands it over to me. "Kenneth and I are going to go check on the boys." Maria looks at Kenneth, giving him a look that makes it obvious she expects him to follow her upstairs.

I curiously watch them go, wondering what's inside the letter. Obviously, it's something personal enough that they want me to read it alone. I tuck my finger in the seam of the envelope, flipping the top part of it open.

Inside of it sits a handwritten letter.

I unfold the piece of paper, my eyes instantly trained on Maverick's name on the bottom.

Whatever this is, it's from Maverick.

My eyes scan over his written words.

Dear Mr. and Mrs. Liams,

You don't know me, but I recently came into possession of items I think you might be interested in. You might be wondering why a delivery driver just showed up at your workplace with six random boxes, but I promise you I think you will prize what's inside them.

In the boxes are paintings that somebody very close to me created. They mean a lot to me, and I think they'll mean a lot to you as well. You see, the person who painted these is a girl I think I'm in love with. A girl that your son, Connor, was also in love with. Her name is Veronica Cunningham.

She painted these in a very vulnerable moment for her. It was the night she came clean to me about what happened to your son. I need to add before I continue any further that I am so very sorry about what happened. Hearing Veronica talk about your son let me know that he was a very special young man. But I also gathered that she holds a lot of guilt for what happened to your son, and to be honest, it's killing me to see her live like this.

If there is any part of you that doesn't blame her for what happened to your son, I beg you to look at the paintings she recently completed. And I mean really look at them, because if you do, I think you'll also see how truly and utterly sorry she is for her part in what happened to Connor.

So, please, look at these paintings with the mentality that she loved your son with every part of her, and know that she is still devastated by what happened to him.

Please look at them and find forgiveness for her, because I don't think she's realized this yet, but she needs that from you more than she would ever admit.

Now, it kind of pains me to do this because I don't know what kind of people you are, and I didn't buy these paintings just so they could be a talking piece at some rich folks' boring dinners, but I want you to do with these paintings as you wish.

Part of me hopes you'll keep at least two of them, and the other part hopes you'll auction off the rest to earn money for the charity in Connor's name. I've done a lot of research on everything your organization has done, and it's something I would love to donate to in Veronica's name.

Please don't tell Veronica I contacted you. I know she will probably figure it out for herself, but I don't want her to think I did this to get her to love me back. I didn't even really do it for her, I did it for your son. I did it for Connor. Because he and I apparently have a lot in common. He loved Veronica truly, madly, deeply; I can tell just from the way she talks about him. And I want to make sure his death makes a difference. Because I am also truly, madly, deeply in love with the woman he loved, and I want to make sure their love lives on through his charity.

So, do with these paintings as you will. They are yours now. Just please, make sure Veronica finds a way to forgive herself. And please, make sure whoever buys these paintings truly appreciates them.

Maverick

I READ over the letter three times before I finally set it down on the coffee table in front of me.

Fucking Maverick.

I can't handle him.

I don't know what to do with his love for me—but I know I won't turn it away again.

I don't know how I've been lucky enough to have not one, but *two* selfless men love me, but I won't take it for granted twice.

So, for once, when I decide to run, I run *toward* someone instead of away from them.

I exchange goodbyes with the Liams, and then with my parents, and I book the first flight back to Kansas, even though it's the day before New Year's Eve and the airport is bound to be packed.

This time, nothing will stop me from fighting for the man I love.

42

MAVERICK

OUR HOUSE IS FILLED to the brim with drunk twenty-some-things. Aspen and I have very different definitions on what a *small get together* is, but here I am, on New Year's Eve, avoiding people in my own backyard. It's cold enough that I can see my breath each time I breathe out.

It's almost midnight and I wish I was beginning the new year with Veronica by my side. It's been over a month since she fled from me—from *us*—and the wound still hurts. I still miss her.

I wish she wasn't halfway across the country from me tonight.

The Liams called a week ago.

They told me how much Veronica's paintings raised for Connor's Ocean. I had to brace myself against the kitchen counter when I heard the total.

She did that.

Her *work* did that for Connor.

I was so proud of her. I was too nervous to ask if she had attended the function or not, but luckily, Maria loves to talk. She told me Veronica was there when they were auctioned off, and that she took it well. That she was thankful and that she seemed *happy*.

I was happy she was happy, I just wished her happiness included me.

But if she's happy there, if she's healing, I'm grateful for that. She deserves to get rid of the guilt. To move on.

I'm very fortunate to have had Lily through all this. My sister sucks at keeping secrets, and since she's been keeping in touch with Veronica, I've been receiving small updates from her on how Veronica is doing.

Just the other night I was hanging out with Selma, Aspen, and Lily, when both Lily and Selma were swearing Veronica would be back. That we would be together once she's had her time. I felt hope when I heard it from their lips, but I tried not to let that hope take over.

I've never met a healed version of Veronica, and once she is healed—if she heals—I'm not confident she'd want to come back to this small college town and give me a real chance.

I hear the sound of the back door opening and closing, but I don't look that way. I'm too focused on dwelling in my feelings for Veronica.

There's the sound of boots crunching against snow.

And I look in the direction of the noise—my eyes landing on a pair of boots I could never forget. My gaze travels up her breathtaking body as Veronica comes face-to-face with me.

"You know I don't like being ignored." Her blue eyes focus on my face.

We both take the moment to stare at each other. Even though it's only been a month, I feel like I need to be reacquainted with her entire *being*.

Those high cheekbones with the tiny freckles that my lips have memorized.

Her lips that are the perfect shade of pink and always look swollen.

Her eyes, that used to scream sadness, but are now more mellow. Calm.

"I'm pissed at you, you know," I say. The words sound strange coming from my throat. Gravelly, quiet. I'm still trying to process the fact that she's standing right across from me.

"Yeah, well I seem to do that a lot for people," she says.

The fog from her breath mixes with the fog of mine. They

dance together in perfect harmony. Harmony I wish Veronica and I could have.

"Wrong answer," I say.

Her body twitches with my words. She shuffles her feet in the snow, as if she's nervous right now. "What are you talking about?"

"I want you to ask *why* I'm pissed at you."

She lets out a long sigh. "Why are you pissed at me, Maverick?"

"I'm pissed at you because I've thought about this a lot and I think your whole ice queen thing comes from the fact that you don't want people to leave you. Even though it wasn't his fault, Connor left. And since then, you've been telling this lie to yourself that if you don't let people get close enough to you to leave, then all will be well in your world. But you didn't think about one thing when you devised that stupid plan in your head," I tell her.

She looks me dead in the eye as she says, "Oh yeah and what's that?"

"Me."

"You?"

I take a step closer to her, my hand slowly reaching out to play with a strand of her hair that has fallen out of her ponytail. "Yes, me. Because I am in love with you, consequences be damned. I am in love with you no matter what I face because, Veronica, I am going to stay. I am going to stay and fucking love you through it. It might be ugly at points, but I want to stay through it all because the thought of not having you isn't an option for me. I'm pissed at you because you up and left before I could prove to you that I would stay with you regardless of what you threw at me. Just when I was given the opportunity to prove to you that I was serious in my pursuit of pursuing you forever, you left. Not even giving me the chance to show you I would fucking stay if you would just *let me*."

Veronica leans into my touch, her eyes staring at my lips.

I remember the time I asked her why she was always staring at my lips and she confessed it was because of the scar. A scar Lily gave me when she threw her Barbie's pink car at my face.

"Is that all?" she asks, leaning away enough from my hand to look me in the eye.

"No, it isn't. I'm also *proud* of you. The more time I had to think about it, the more I was happy you ran home. Because for me to love you the way you *deserve* to be loved, I needed you to pick up your own pieces. To heal some on your own. I've learned a lot because of my last relationship and I learned I can't be the white knight for the girl I love. I don't want to be that again. I want to be your sidekick, not your hero. I'm proud of you for going home and facing everything that came with that and I hope that maybe one day, when you feel like you can open your heart again without having all the guilt, that maybe I can have a chance."

I take a breath and add, "I saw something once that said you can't be loved by someone until you love yourself and I still think it's bullshit. I get that you don't like yourself. You've made some mistakes in your life and now you have to live with them. I still don't think Connor's death was your fault, and I hope you realized that while home. But I am telling you right now that you don't have to love yourself. You don't even have to like yourself, because I love you enough for the both of us. I didn't expect it to happen, I don't even know how it happened, but it did.

"And now I will show you just how worthy of love you are despite every shitty thing that has happened to you and *especially* after every shitty thing you have done. I love you despite all of it. One of these days, my love will show you that it's okay to love yourself, too—despite your flaws, *because* of your flaws. Because I am in love with every single thing that makes you *you*. The good, the bad, the ugly. All of it. So, once you've picked up your pieces, once you can love again, even if it isn't by loving yourself, I want you to choose me." I cup both of her cheeks in my hand, pulling her face to look up at me.

I want her to see the sincerity in my eyes. I want her to know I love her, despite everything that's happened. But I also want her to know I won't rush her. When she accepts us—*if she accepts us*—I need her to know it will mean forever for me. However long she lets our forever be.

"Are you going to give me the opportunity to talk or are you going to continue to give speeches?" She playfully bumps her nose against mine, her legs stretching so she can reach my face.

I laugh, white air bursting from my mouth with the action. "I'm all ears."

"'Kay, thanks," Veronica responds, reaching up to wrap her small fingers around mine.

Her hand is surprisingly warm in the frigid temperature.

"Maverick," she begins, looking up at me. Snow has started to fall, and it catches on her long eyelashes. She tries to blink it away, but it continues to cling to them. "When we first met, I was basically a shell of a person. I hated myself so much that there wasn't really anything else to me. I pushed people away like it was my job. I wasn't ready to open myself up to another person, let alone give myself to them. But it was different with you. I thought you were safe because you were with Selma. It turns out I was slowly giving away pieces of myself to you unintentionally.

"And when I was hundreds of miles away from you, I wanted to *intentionally* give the rest of myself to you. Because when I saw my paintings on that stage, raising money for Connor's Ocean, my head realized what my heart already knew. It knew I needed you. It knew that you made me a better person, that you made me not just *want* to be better, but actually *be* better.

"You inspired me to figure my shit out. That's what I've been doing for the last month. Since I last saw you, I've been talking about my problems, facing the Liams, and even bonding with my parents. I still have so much to work on. You'll get annoyed with me, I promise. I'm still selfish, I can still act like a child, and I still can't figure out why you and Aspen are so close, but if you'll have me, I want to give this another shot." She places her tiny hand over my chest.

My thick jacket must be in the way, however, because she slowly brings the zipper down. Veronica flattens her palm right above my heart. I can feel the heat of her hand through the thin fabric of my shirt. I would bet money that she could feel the beat of my heart against that small hand. My heart is trying to beat its way out of my chest and land right in her hand.

She already owns it anyway.

"The pieces of my heart love the pieces of your heart. And I was wondering if, as we both fix ourselves, we could maybe mix our pieces together?" Her fingers nervously drum against my chest, something I often find myself doing when I'm nervous.

I open my mouth to say something, but both our heads turn to the house when we hear the chanting from the house. It must be almost midnight because there is the sound of people counting down as the ball begins to drop.

"Ten...nine...eight...seven..."

Veronica lifts up on her toes, so she is face-to-face with me. "I love you with everything I have, Maverick Morrison."

And as the clock strikes midnight, I start the new year with Veronica's lips against mine.

It's *perfect*.

We hear people cheering inside. Lily even sticks her head out to yell obscenities at us as we continue to make out. I have my fingers threaded through the strands of Veronica's ponytail, pulling her close to me like I'm a starved man—and I feel like one. Snow has continued to fall around us, leaving small wet spots all over both of us.

"I love you, too," I tell her. And I do—despite her pushing me away, despite the consequences. I love her.

Best of all, she managed to fall in love with me, too.

EPILOGUE

VERONICA

THE WATER IS cold against my toes. I yelp once it begins to brush against my thighs.

Maverick laughs next to me, and I look over at him. His skin is the perfect shade of golden tan after we've spent our summer here in South Carolina.

We've been together a year and a half now. A year and a half that was filled with ups and downs—but ups and downs we conquered *together*.

Maverick graduated last summer, pre-law. I was terrified he would move far away, and I would've moved anywhere with him, but we both wanted to end up in the same place.

Here—in South Carolina.

Instead of being a criminal defense lawyer, Maverick decided he wanted to pursue his dream of helping people through pro-bono opportunities. So, he just changed his direction on *how* exactly he would do that. Now, he's in his first year of law school to become an attorney for nonprofits. He plans to open his own practice here in South Carolina.

His first client will be Connor's Ocean.

Maverick and I both wanted to spend a summer here to make sure living in South Carolina is what we really want. We figured out in the first week that *this* is where both of us need to be.

Now that I've graduated with a marketing degree, I'm the new marketing director for Connor's Ocean. It allows me to continue to paint and let my creative side out, while also making a difference in something that's important to me.

"What are you thinking about?" Maverick's voice covers the sound of the crashing waves.

I look at him. The man I am so hopelessly in love with.

I plan to marry him one day. That one day may be sooner rather than later considering Lily spilled the beans that he was out looking for rings recently.

We don't have the most conventional of love stories, but it's *ours*.

"Just how we got to be here," I answer him.

"In South Carolina?" he questions, his feet kicking up water as he walks toward me.

I gladly walk right into his strong arms, allowing him to wrap his arms around me. I tuck my head under his jaw. "Yeah. When I lost Connor years ago, I never thought I would willingly choose to come back to South Carolina. But here I am, *happy* to be moving back. Happy to be starting a new chapter—with you. I don't know what I would've done without you, Mav." I nestle closer into his chest as he squeezes me tighter.

"You would have been fine without me," he says. "It may have taken a bit longer, but you're strong, you would have figured it out—with or without me. I am happy that life played out the way it did though, because you're my world." He presses his lips against my hair.

"I think Connor would've really liked you," I say, pointing my head to look up at him.

There's clear emotion on his face, his Adam's apple bobbing up and down in his throat. "I think he would be very proud of you, Veronica."

"Yeah," I say, looking out at the ocean. "I think he would be, too."

The ocean continues to crash around us as we both stay locked in our moment.

The sun breaks through the clouds, and if I believed in

something beyond this life we live, I would think that maybe Connor is looking down upon us. I'm unsure about my thoughts of the afterlife, but I take comfort that, regardless, the sun has begun to shine on my life again.

So, as I press my face against Maverick's neck, I think about the first boy who taught me about life. The boy that I lost way too soon, but the boy I will continue to try and make proud.

Even though Connor is no longer with us, his spirit lives on in the charity work we do, and it makes me content to know he has been immortalized through Connor's Ocean.

I think back to the girl I was when I was with Connor.

I had spent so much of my time loving him, even after he was gone, that I didn't know who I was without the love I had for him and the guilt I held for his death. It was during a therapy session that I realized I had tangled those feelings up too much.

I had to unravel them piece by piece.

I kept the love I had for Connor deep in my heart, a love I would never let go of.

But I got rid of the guilt. Maverick helped me do that.

I think about the man who brought me back to life after losing the boy I loved. The man who stopped *me* from drowning. The man whose arms are wrapped around me right now, still protecting me from my own waves.

I didn't think I would ever be ready to fall in love again when I met Maverick, but it turns out for the right man, I was.

He's taught me so much in the year and a half we've been together. He's taught me how to fight my own battles—instead of doing it for me.

On days it's hard to love myself, he gives me reminders.

On days I *know* I'm being difficult, he doesn't falter.

I look out at the ocean when I think about everything that has happened in my twenty-two years of life.

I've been through some traumatic things—but I survived them.

Not only did I survive them, but I found happiness afterward.

"I love you, Maverick."

"I love you, too."

We both stare out at the ocean as the wave wraps around our feet, carrying the last of my guilt with it when it retreats.

ACKNOWLEDGMENTS

Okay, I need a minute here. IS THIS ACTUALLY HAPPEN-ING? If you're reading this, it means you have made it to the very end of my book baby and I need a hot minute to let that soak in. Is this real life? I still can't believe this. While I'm stuck in perpetual shock that my debut is officially out into the world, I need to thank numerous people for getting me here. I couldn't have done it without so many rad people behind me.

First, my husband. When I told you I wanted to write a book, you didn't look at me like I was crazy. There were so many nights I wasn't present because I couldn't get these characters out of my head. You put up with it like a champ and always supported me in following my dream. You also suffered through the MANY car rides where I obsessively listened to TCOLM's playlist. For that, I thank you. Especially because I know some of the songs that inspired this story really aren't your jam. I love you with everything I have. You are my very own book boyfriend. Thank you.

Mom, I have no idea if you'll be reading this. Part of me hopes you won't because well...there's sex. *Awkward*. But if you are...hi, Mom! You are my biggest hero. My forever role model. You've given me the world, and I hope to give a fraction of that back to you someday. I love you.

Courtney, where the hell do I even start with you? I didn't

know we would become such smutty soul sisters—but we did—and you are stuck with me forever. You've read all the words I've ever written (even when they sucked) and I appreciate you so much. Your dedication to my words and characters have always meant so much to me. Thank you for always being my biggest fan. I love your ass so much.

Christina, you are like a magical fucking fairy godmother who took this book in its rawest form and helped me polish it into something I'm so proud of. I will never be able to thank you for taking me on as a debut author even though I suck at using contractions and I could write a whole paragraph before I end the damn sentence. You always made me feel like I was important to you and that my book mattered, and that means the world to me. Thank you. Will you be my editor forever and ever? I won't let you leave me.

To my betas. Y'all got this book when it still needed a LOT of work and you still loved it hard. Tasha, you gave me inspiration for one of my favorite scenes with the spin the bottle suggestion and I loved the way it played out. You rock. Thank you. *The Consequence of Loving Me* could be so different (and not in a great way) if it weren't for you ladies. So many thanks to all of you and your ideas that helped make this book the way it is.

Ashlee, Ashlee, Ashlee, you fucking teaser and trailer rockstar. You understood my vision and aesthetic for this book when I only gave you small fragments of it. You are so badass and I'm so lucky to call you a friend now, too. You're fucking stuck with me. THANK YOU.

Kat Savage, you gave me advice more times than I can even count. It was so touching that a successful author like you would take the time out of their day to help me navigate the waters of self-publishing. Thank you, thank you, thank you.

To the bloggers and bookstagrammers out there. There are so many I could name here. You guys deserve all the praise in the world. I developed my passion for writing after sitting on the sidelines for so long as a blogger myself. I know the passion and dedication you put into each and every picture, post, and review you share on social media. I know the vast amount of book options out there, so the fact that you chose to read *my* words with your precious reading time is so humbling. Keep being badass out there; as an author, I appreciate it so much.

Last, but not freaking least, to the readers. I know the risk you take when reading a novel from a debut author. Thank you for trusting me enough to read the words I so desperately wanted to share with the world. I will never be able to explain how much it means to me. I will continue to pour my heart into the stories I want to create as a thank you.

PINTEREST BOARD AND SPOTIFY PLAYLIST

Pinterest Board:
http://bit.ly/tcolmpinterest

Spotify Playlist:
http://bit.ly/tcolmplaylist

ABOUT THE AUTHOR

Kat Singleton lives in the Midwest with her husband and their two very lazy doodles. Before she ever wrote her first words, she was a book blogger who fell in love with reading at a young age. In her spare time, you can find her surviving off iced coffee and sneaking in a few pages of her current read. Being an author was a dream of hers—for years and years. She's excited that dream has now become a reality.

CONTACT

Email: authorkatsingleton@gmail.com
Website: authorkatsingleton.com
Facebook: Author Kat Singleton
Instagram: authorkatsingleton
Facebook Reader Group: Kat Singleton's Sweethearts
Free Download: *The Waves of Wanting You*

ALSO BY KAT SINGLETON

The Road to Finding Us

Printed in Great Britain
by Amazon